GANGSTER SCHOOL

KATE WISEMAN

A Middle Grade Comic Adventure Story

Copyright © Kate Wiseman 2018

First published in 2018 by
ZunTold

www.zuntold.com

Cover designed by Isla Bousfield-Donohoe

British Library Cataloguing-in-Publication data
A catalogue record for this book is available from the British Library

ISBN: 978-1-9998633-1-9

Printed and bound in the UK by Short Run Press

For Frank and Harry, with love.

Praise for *Gangster School*

A masterly mayhem of an adventure!
– *Book Lover Jo*

Bonkers, full of hilarious little moments of
gigglesome humour and feels fresh and unique.
– *ReaditDaddy*

Highly recommend this fun and really original story.
Milly, Charlie and Gruffles will become your
new best friends.
– *Mike Reads*

Gangster School is exactly what middle-grade should be:
full of friendship and mayhem and children
questioning their identity. It's criminally good.
– *Book Murmuration*

ACKNOWLEDGEMENTS

There are numerous people who deserve my undying thanks for helping me to become a *Published Author*: to Frank and Harry, for believing in me even when I didn't, and for laughing at my jokes. Penny Blackmore, thanks for the wildly creative lunches, only slightly helped along by prosecco. To Tamsyn Murray, mentor extraordinaire, thanks for sharing your wisdom, patience, insights and experience. To Ben Illis, fab agent, thanks so much for your wisdom and endless enthusiasm. Oh, and my sunglasses ARE genuine! Probably. To my publisher at ZunTold, Elaine Bousfield, thanks a million for your belief in Gangster School and your enormous patience. I'd say thanks to my cats for all the encouraging cuddles when I got stuck, but you'd think I was strange. And anyway, they can't read.

CHAPTER ONE

Milly could stand it no longer. She strode up to the tall boy who was completely engrossed in the game he was playing on his mobile, and poked him in the ribs with her rolled-up school prospectus.

'You. You *do* know your pocket's being picked, don't you?'

The boy gaped at her before dragging the headphones off his mop of hair and swivelling round to look behind him.

A cherubic-looking toddler in a teddy bear coat had levered herself onto her tip toes in order to wriggle one hand into the back pocket of the boy's jeans. When she realised she'd been rumbled, the moppet snatched back her hand and stomped over to a group of grown-ups, who'd been watching with indulgent smiles.

'Good try, Isla, I'm proud of you,' said a man who must be the toddler's father. Isla poked her tongue out at the girl who'd thwarted her crime. The girl stared back for a few seconds, then turned her back on her.

'Crikey! Thanks. Maybe I should stay on my toes,' said the boy.

'Maybe you should. This is Blaggard's, remember. I'm Milly, by the way, Milly Dillane. That's M-I-L-L-Y. Who are you?'

The boy looked a little surprised at Milly's directness. 'I'm Charlie. Charlie Partridge. Great to meet you.'

'Tell me something, Charlie,' Milly said. 'Has your dog read the prospectus?'

Charlie looked blank, so Milly tried again: 'It *does* know that it can't come with you?' She straightened out the thick wad of paper. 'Look at this: *'Pets are strictly forbidden at Blaggard's. Criminal masterminds are supposed to be heartless loners. You won't scare anyone if you're mooning over a fluffy kitten,'* she read.

Charlie looked down at the dog. It seemed to be glued to his leg. It was whitish, curly-haired and, putting it politely, it smelt powerfully. Its eyes never budged from Charlie's face. 'Yeah. You know that, don't you, Gruffles? He's not happy about it though.'

'Gruffles? Great name... Poodle?' Milly examined the dog with interest.

'No. He's a – actually, I don't really know.' Charlie frowned as he looked at his pet. 'A spaniel with some beagle mixed in. Probably. Maybe.'

'A Spangle! That explains his patches. I thought it was odd, having a patchy poodle!'

There was a short silence as they both stared at the dog. 'He hasn't got any patches. He's white all over. It's mud... I hope.'

Milly took a deep sniff and wrinkled her nose. Charlie followed suit and fanned the air in front of his face with his hand. Milly's lips twitched. She started to laugh. A second later, Charlie joined in. 'I don't know why he smells so bad. My mum's always bathing him. He hates it,' he said.

As he spoke, Charlie gestured towards his parents – a short woman in a white suit and a much taller man. They were among a group of gossiping adults waiting outside a pair of huge gates that were giving off an electrical buzz.

At first glance, the gates looked like upright muddles of metallic spaghetti, but when you looked closer, you began to make out shapes in them. There were snarling bear heads – at least a dozen – scattered between poison ivy leaves. The borders looked a lot like clumps of stinging nettles.

A bell inside the school grounds began tolling nine. The chatter stopped and all eyes swivelled towards the gates. As the final chime rang out, a tall woman in a grey trouser suit appeared. She prowled down a tree-lined path, stopped at the gates and punched some numbers into a keypad. The gates slid apart, their steeliness mirrored in the woman's watchful eyes. Her glossy brown hair was shot through with streaks of grey. She stalked into the middle of the crowd and tapped her foot as she waited for the spurt of spontaneous applause to die.

'Thank you. Welcome.' Her voice was deep and throaty, almost a purr. 'I'm Griselda Martinet, the Head Teacher. Students, it's time to take your first steps through our infamous Twisted Gates. I'll wait for you inside. Say your goodbyes and join me.'

She walked a short distance away, then stopped in a patch of sunlight just inside the grounds and stretched in the warmth. Charlie gave his parents swift hugs and a longer one to his dog. He and Milly joined the crowd jostling through the Twisted Gates to the accompaniment of Gruffles' howls.

In front of them were dense woods, with a path cutting through them towards a distant building. Its long, thatched roof was just visible above the tree line. The pair chatted as they edged towards the Head Teacher. 'Your parents not here?' the boy enquired.

'No. They offered to come, but I thought they'd get upset. Dad, especially!' The girl rolled her eyes. As they caught up with Ms Martinet, a distant but spectacular yowl from Gruffles reached their ears.

The Head Teacher walked beside them, smiling. 'Dogs! So pathetically devoted! He'll get over it, eventually... On to more interesting things.' Turning to face the crowd of children following her, she called out in a loud voice, 'firstly, remember that outside of Blaggard's you must, if you value your kneecaps, refer to the school by its cover identity – Constance Bottomley's Academy for the Rural Arts. The Dependable public – all those tedious, law-abiding citizens – *MUST* remain ignorant of our real identity. From now on, the less you have to do with Dependables, the better.

'Now, a little chat about the school uniform. I expect you can't wait to get into it. The stripy burglar's jumper, even a black mask for formal occasions! Your first chance to look like real criminals. Who's just *itching* to put it on?'

A dozen eager hands shot into the air. Ms Martinet smiled.

'That's just lovely. And I'm sure you'll look marvelous in it. *BUT! Never. Ever.* Wear your uniform outside the school gates. The reason should be obvious. Do I make myself *ab-so-lutely* clear?' There was no trace of a smile now. Her eyes had narrowed and they were glittering like icicles in winter sunshine.

Milly and Charlie took an involuntary step backwards. Ms Martinet opened her mouth to say more, but at that moment a woman hurried out of the woods. She caught her foot in a tree root and stumbled. Her face flushed and a look of thunder descended over it. She was a good bit younger than Ms Martinet and she was wearing a prim grey dress. Her hair was pulled into a bun that was so tight it looked as if her eyes would pop out of their sockets.

'Head Teacher I would apologise for this interruption, if politeness was in my nature. As it isn't, I'll simply say that your presence is required NOW. A group of Year Nines has captured Mr Molesworthy. They've squeezed him into the safe used for bank-robbing practise and they're refusing to let him out until he gives them the combination for the school strongbox. There's not much air in there – the safe I mean. There's probably even less in the strongbox.'

Ms Martinet sighed. 'Very well, Miss Vipond. New Blaggardians, wait here. I'll be back soon. Just remain alert and bear in mind the addendum in your prospectus...' She hurried away with the angry looking woman scurrying after her.

The new Blaggardians huddled together and peered through the gloomy trees. 'What's an addendum when it's at home?' Charlie said.

Milly flicked through the pages of the prospectus. A tiny slip of paper fluttered to the ground. She picked it up, squinting as she read it aloud.

'Got it! *It's a cherished tradition at Blaggard's for the Year Eights to ambush the new Year Sevens, in order to relieve them of their precious possessions. Custom dictates that this is undertaken within the first hour of their arrival at the school. New students are therefore asked to ensure that laptops, phones, etc are sent to the school ahead of them.'*

Her final words were lost. Whooping and hollering, a mass of savages in black masks and striped tops pounced from behind the trees, throwing themselves onto the newbies. 'This is great! Five minutes at Blaggard's and they've mugged us,' Charlie groaned.

CHAPTER TWO

T he triumphant Year Eights prodded their captives on a twisted route through the trees. A couple of minutes later they were lining them up against an old white wall. 'This must be the back of the main building,' Milly muttered to Charlie.

With what seemed like practised efficiency, the Year Eights split into two groups. The largest band stayed with their captives, looming over them and snarling at them to keep them intimidated. The rest set about relieving them of anything that looked expensive. Milly was at the end of the line. She raised her eyebrows as Charlie slipped his mobile into his sock, then hung on to his laptop bag for dear life as two ambushers tried to wrestle it from him.

Some of the Year Sevens tried to dissuade them. One, a short, sturdy boy with freckles, tried reasoning with his captors. 'Now let's just stop and think about what you're doing here. Have you taken into account that this could easily go disastrously wrong? A much more successful approach would be to....'

Milly didn't waste her breath. She was scanning her surroundings with narrowed eyes. 'Newbies, grab your stuff and follow me!' she yelled suddenly, shoving the nearest pair of Year Eights backwards. Clutching her belongings, she ran.

The other Year Sevens hesitated for a second and then most of them – maybe thirty – followed. Glancing over her shoulder, Milly saw Charlie frowning after her. Then he, too, took to his heels. The robbers stared blankly at each other before launching into a chase. A few stayed behind with the stragglers.

The Year Sevens rounded a corner. Milly stopped, scanning the long wall in front of them. It was dotted with five identical doors. Each one was arched, with corroded metal hinges and hefty doorknobs. For a second she calculated. She risked another quick look behind her, to see whether the rest of the newbies were following. No one appeared. Shrugging, she set off again. She reached the door on the far left and shoved it, hard. It gave a stubborn creak and refused to budge.

'Charlie. Here, now. I need you,' Milly threw the words behind her. He was there in a second, adding his shoulders to the force pitted against the door. It gave way with a long g-r-o-a-n. They dashed inside and then stopped, temporarily blinded by the sudden darkness.

They were in a gloomy corridor, ending in a dappled glass door. As Milly's eyes adjusted, she began to make out the long, dark tables and shelf-lined walls in the room beyond the door. Everything was distorted by the glass. An unmistakable chemical aroma seeped into the air.

'Great! Come on,' Milly yelled. She shoved open the door and bundled the Year Sevens inside. Down the corridor, the outside door crashed open again. Year Eights streamed through. They too stopped for a second while their eyes adjusted.

Milly scanned the room. Lining one side there was a row of skeletons in order of size, ranging from a delicate bat to a sturdy rhino. The smallest ones were suspended from the ceiling.

Along the back wall were jars of chemicals. Most of them were green or blue or brown, but on the highest shelf were a cluster of black ones, with red grinning skulls pressed into the glass. Milly's eyes passed over them and onto a poster. They returned to it briefly to reread the title – *Banish Early Bedtimes – Drug Your Parents!* She raised one eyebrow.

Just along from the poster, ranks of yellow biohazard suits hung from their pegs like a dormant alien army. Once again, Milly's eyes moved on. Finally she spotted something that might be helpful. Tucked away in a corner was a row of metal canisters on a high shelf. She sprinted over to them and craned on tiptoe to read their labels. 'Charlie, come here! I'm too short. Read these to me.'

Charlie hesitated for a moment. The sound of their pursuers hurtling through the laboratory door seemed to jolt him into action, and in two seconds flat he was at Milly's side. 'What did your last slave die of?' he said, with a quick smile.

He reached up for the nearest canister. 'Instant spray

ice. For outdoor use only,' he read out. 'Could we run off and make a skid patch behind us?'

Milly shook her head. 'Can't risk it. Some of us would end up skidding on it, too.'

He threw it down and reached for the next one. '*Fake blood. Spray onto injury-free areas and groan loudly.* Useless!' He tossed it to one side and grabbed another one. *Temporary paralysis gas. For use on Dependables in criminal enterprises only. Hold your breath for 30 seconds after spraying.*'

Milly punched the air. 'YES! Pass that to me.' She shook the canister. 'Argh! It's half empty. Is there any more?'

'There's one more and it *looks* the same, but the label's gone. Could be anything.'

'Cross your fingers that it *is* the same. Everyone, hold your breath. Keep together. Don't breathe till we're outside.'

Milly aimed the unlabelled canister at the Year Eights, who were almost within grabbing distance. She took a step back and punched down on the nozzle. A hissing purple cloud enveloped the ambushers. For a second there was silence. And then the gang of muggers began to laugh. They guffawed and hooted. They clutched at tables or each other to stop themselves from collapsing.

'Laughing gas! That won't stop them for long.' She tossed the canister to one side. She grabbed the half-empty one, gave it a quick shake and squirted the chortling Year Eights with yellow vapour. Instantly they froze, caught in mid-hoot. It was a disturbing sight – as if the victims of the Pompeii volcano were delighted at their grisly fate.

'Wish there was time to take a few photos to post on

Crimbook, but we need air,' Milly gasped as she hustled the bulgy-eyed Year Sevens back into the clean sunshine.

'That was great, Milly.' Charlie was clutching his knees, gulping down air. 'You're new too, aren't you – how'd you know where to find that science lab?'

Milly shrugged. 'I had a good look at the map of the school this morning – the one in the prospectus. This is Blaggard's. Weird stuff happens. You need to be ready for it.' She smiled up into his brown eyes.

Ms Martinet returned to find most of the new Blaggardians where she'd left them, panting and dishevelled. She threw them a knowing look.

'Well done for fighting off the Year Eights. I assume your less successful classmates have been released by now. They'll be waiting for us by the main door.' She shepherded them onwards.

'Don't even think about retaliation, by the way,' she warned. 'There's a strict Honour Among Thieves policy at Blaggard's. We allow the Year Eight Ambush because it's a centuries old tradition, but that's as far as it goes. *Ab-so-lutely* no other criminal activities are permitted against fellow pupils.' She gave the Year Sevens a steely-eyed glare. 'Understood?'

The newbies nodded feverishly.

'Excellent. Now follow me,' she purred.

CHAPTER THREE

The woods gave way to slightly overgrown lawns. Dotted at intervals around this natural boundary were half a dozen outbuildings – some looking like sheds, while others had curtains and painted doors, like homely cottages. But Milly's eyes were drawn to the main building. It had the thick, black and white half-timber walls of a quaint Tudor cottage, but it was built on an enormous scale, spreading upwards and outwards in every direction. *Kind of like a cross between an olde inne and a presidential palace*, Milly thought.

Standing at either end of the thatched roof were towering statues of rearing bears, made from the same material. Just as Milly was thinking that all that was needed to complete the picture of rural bliss was a flock of sheep nibbling the lawns, a shaft of September sunlight caught a spot of red – no, two spots of red – in the face of the nearest bear. She nudged Charlie and pointed.

'Did you see that? That bear has red eyes.'

Charlie peered upwards. 'Oh, yeah. Security cameras.

We've got something similar at home. Not in bear statues, though. Look! Their heads move round too, so they can check out the whole area. Never seen that before!'

He returned to inspecting the massive, studded front door. 'That looks like it could have been pinched from the Tower of London.'

'It probably was. Sir Thomas Blaggard, the school's founder, was famous for not wasting money if he could steal something instead.' Milly said. She thought about it and added: 'And anyway I expect he'd want to set a bad example.'

As Ms Martinet had predicted, the rest of the Year Sevens were waiting by the door. There were half a dozen of them, some trying to control their trembling lips, others hunching their shoulders and kicking angrily at the wood. Ms Martinet gave them a small, sympathetic smile.

She paused with one foot on the shallow steps that led up to the door. 'Before we cross Blaggard's threshold you need to be aware of something important. In our prospectus we make a simple promise: **Future Infamy Assured**. That means we guarantee to make you into famous villains. Any student who is unwilling or unable to live up to this will be expelled faster than a Fabrication teacher can make up a fib.

'Blaggard's rejects always end up in Crumley's School for Career Criminals, where they don't last long. Crumley's prides itself on turning out the most unpleasant felons in the world. The survival rate amongst Crumleians is something like fifty per cent. Think Criminal, and you won't be adding to that statistic.'

At the mention of Crumley's, the Year Sevens moved closer together. Charlie leant over and muttered to Milly: 'Yikes! Being sent to Crumley's is a fate *worse* than death. Got to avoid that!'

'Yep. That's something we *really*–'

Griselda Martinet's deep voice interrupted her. 'The short girl with the attitude and the tall boy with the hair – I'm usually all in favour of talking over the teacher, as long as that teacher isn't me. As it *is* me, I'd like to suggest that you SHUT UP and pay attention. Wonderful. Now, come in.'

As she was speaking she punched the buttons on another keypad. The door didn't swing open, as Milly had expected; instead it slid sideways and disappeared into a thin recess.

The Reception area at Blaggard's was a spacious, white room. Spotlights were embedded in the ceiling, between timber beams. There was a row of pristine armchairs pushed against one wall, opposite a cabinet crammed with trophies and framed certificates.

The floor was made from tiny mosaic tiles in black, white, silver and gold. Milly examined the circular design with interest. It looked as if people had been working on it for centuries.

In the centre was what seemed to be the oldest part. It depicted Blaggardians in striped doublets and ruffs, shinning up ropes into castles and relieving knights of their armour and horses. Around these were Victorian Blaggardians in black and white frock coats, attaching sticks of dynamite to safes or holding up steam trains. Others carried victims into closed carriages. The newest parts of the design were around the edges. In these, the Blaggardians wore modern uniform and they worked at computers, or stole missiles, or dragged their enemies into sleek cars and armoured vans.

A muscular receptionist sat at a black marble desk, frowning at a bank of video monitors that Milly could easily imagine guarding the Bank of England. On one side of the desk was a tall vase, filled with a bouquet of holly leaves and deadly nightshade.

Dotted around the room were a number of unusual portraits. Taking pride of place on the wall behind the desk was a detailed sketch of a snub-nosed man with a pudding-bowl haircut. Above the man's head were the words:

WANTED – 100 GROAT REWARD!

Beneath the portrait was golden placard reading: '*Sir Thomas Blaggard, Our Beloved Founder – His First Wanted Poster*.' Just to one side of this there was a frayed noose in a glass case. There was a light above it, illuminating the rusty blood that speckled it.

'That's the noose that finished off Sir Thomas. His reward had increased a lot by then,' Milly murmured to Charlie. He wrinkled his nose.

To the left of the noose was a painting of a peachy-cheeked man, waving a lacy hanky. He looked like he'd be more interested in curling his hair than committing villainy. '*Sir Bryon de Bohun – the Devilish Dandy – Our Most Successful Student*', read the sign beneath it. There was a smaller picture beneath Sir Bryon, showing a massive black

15

dog with a pointed snout. According to its little placard this was '*Humbug – Sir Bryon's Attack Dog – 11 confirmed kills.*'

On Sir Thomas' other side was a glowering photo of Griselda Martinet, stretching her sharp-nailed hands towards the photographer. At the top of the photo was a stark message: '*LARGE REWARD! DO NOT APPROACH!*' The little sign beneath the picture read: '*G Martinet – Current Head. (Do NOT reveal her presence here).*' The Year Sevens looked at the Head Teacher in awestruck silence.

Ms Martinet nodded to the receptionist and picked up a pile of papers from the marble desk. She led the new Blaggardians down a corridor towards some stairs. Their deep blue carpet still smelt of newness and Milly breathed in deeply to enjoy it.

Ms Martinet pointed out useful landmarks: 'Girls' changing rooms to the left, boys' to the right. Once you've been here a few months, we'll change your locker combinations regularly to give you some safe-cracking practise. For now, just enter a combination of your choice. And remember – honour among thieves – you WILL NOT break into other students' lockers... Your bedrooms are up these stairs. You'll see them later.'

She handed out the papers she'd collected in Reception.

'Now, here are your timetables. You've got ten minutes to change into your uniforms. Then your criminal education will begin.'

CHAPTER FOUR

'Our first lesson is Thievery,' Milly said to Charlie, after a quick look at her timetable. 'It's one of the compulsory subjects, along with Fabrication, Betrayal, Stealth, Hacking, Plotting and Defiance and Discourtesy. Lots of other choices, too, of course. The timetable was updated recently. No one's interested in Highway Robbery on Horseback and Obtaining Money from Gullible Yokels by Pretending to be a Talking Pig any more.'

'Shame! I've been working on my talking pig skills,' Charlie said, with a grin.

They were in the middle of the gaggle of Year Sevens, tugging at their new striped burglar's tops and adjusting their multi-pocketed trousers as they assembled outside the locker rooms before the lesson. Among the group was a tall, lean girl with a determined chin. She looked a little older than the rest of the group. She'd been one of those who hadn't followed Milly's lead during the Year Eight Ambush.

'I'm Agatha Quint. I'm gonna be a criminal escape specialist. I'll be getting lessons in the holidays from Boneless Brad Cunningham – the world's only one hundred per cent successful escapologist. He's my second cousin. There are loads of escapologists in my family, and I'm gonna be the best of the lot! Look he gave me these handcuffs – they're engraved,' she said, passing them around and pointing to the message – *Agatha – Keep Wriggling! B.B.C.* I've brought lots of other pairs with me. Collecting handcuffs is my hobby!'

'They're cool,' Milly said, passing the handcuffs to Charlie. Do you think you could give me some escapology tips sometime? You never know when they'd be useful.'

Agatha gave her a cool look. 'Sorry. Every crim for themselves.'

Milly raised her eyebrows. 'Pity you haven't started your escapology lessons yet. If you had, you might have got on better in the Ambush,' she retorted. Agatha Quint shot her a look of dislike and turned away.

The Thievery classroom was the first room in one of the corridors branching off from Reception. There was a painting on the door of a masked Blaggardian, tiptoeing away with a brimming bag of loot.

'It says in the prospectus that the classroom doors are decorated with a picture reflecting the subject taught in it. It's to help newbies,' said the freckly boy who'd tried to reason with the Year Eight ambushers. He'd introduced himself as William Proctor.

'This must be it, then,' Milly said, and pushed open the door. The teacher hadn't arrived yet, so the new Blaggardians sat down and looked around them. Apart from a poster *'Bank Vaults of the World and How to Get Into Them'* – and an elaborate wall display headed: *'Inspirational Robbers: Find YOUR Role Model',* the room was beige and bland. They were taking out their pencil cases and crowbars when the door opened just wide enough to allow a figure to slide into the room.

It took several moments for the Year Sevens to realise that they were no longer alone. Milly spotted the man first and nudged Charlie, who'd been assessing the class computer as if it was a priceless painting. The man glided over to Milly and Charlie, who were sitting at the front of the room. 'Welcome to Thievery,' he said, in a flat voice.

Milly looked up at a man with dust-coloured hair and puffy cheeks, like a hamster with half-filled face pouches. He was a little shorter than average height. He was wearing a beige suit that should have made him look smart, but it didn't. 'Thanks, sir,' Milly said, assessing the man with interest. He gave a slight nod and returned to the front of the class. He stood completely still and waited. Soon every head turned his way. He managed a faint smile and began speaking in a finicky voice.

'Good morning, new Blaggardians. I'm Nick Lightfinger and I'm going to be teaching you all there is to know about acquiring items that aren't *officially* yours. The Lightfingers have been experts ever since Thaddeus Lightfinger made off with all the fire extinguishers during the Great Fire of London.'

Somewhere close behind Milly, a girl laughed out loud and said, very clearly, 'Hilarious. My sides are splitting.' The tone of the girl's voice made it clear that she didn't find it funny at all.

Lightfinger looked annoyed. 'Who said that? What makes you think I'm joking? I never joke! Was it you?' he was staring at Milly, pale brows drawn into a straight line. 'It *was* you, wasn't it?'

Milly opened her mouth to deny it, but before she could frame a word Charlie coughed and said in a strangled voice: 'Sorry, Sir. It was me. I was thinking about a joke I heard today, about a-a- short-sighted thief who tried to escape from a yacht he'd been raiding on a shark that he mistook for a plastic inflatable. Every time I remember it, I split my sides laughing. It's hilarious! When I laugh a lot it makes me cough, and that makes my voice go funny.' He coughed a bit more to emphasise his point.

'Very well,' Lightfinger said, after a second or two, 'but you won't get far at Blaggard's if you own up every time you misbehave. And can I suggest that you restrain your appetite for weak jokes until my lesson has finished. A Thievery class is no place for fun!' Charlie gave Milly a wink.

'You can say that again,' he whispered as Lightfinger turned back to the whiteboard and picked up a pen. 'Sorry about the lame joke – it was all I could come up with! I think it was that tall girl with the handcuffs who upset him. Agatha? Maybe she's out to show you up?'

Milly threw a quick glance over her shoulder. For a moment, Agatha Quint met her eyes with a gaze of mild innocence. Then she looked back at the teacher.

'Hmmm. I'll bear that in mind. I could have talked my

way out of that without help, you know. But it's nice to have someone looking out for me, for a change. So thanks.'

'I'm sure you could,' Charlie said apologetically. 'But I had a sudden flash of inspiration. It doesn't happen often, and I didn't want to waste it!'

Clutching the pen in his pudgy hands, Lightfinger was talking again: 'The secret of the Lightfingers' success has always been our ability to blend into the background. Believe me, it's not easy. It takes complete self-control.' A look of pride settled on his plain face. 'Our family motto is *Bland is Best!*'

'Why am I not surprised?' Milly murmured to Charlie, under the pretext of taking a notepad out of her bag. He rolled his eyes at her.

'I've got some very exciting news to announce,' Lightfinger droned on. 'But first, I'm going to give you a few essential tips on keeping your self-control. That's the bedrock of this subject. It needs to be second nature before you even attempt to rearrange the ownership of your desired items. So let's have some ideas on how to develop iron self-control. Hands up.'

'Become a Dependable,' someone called from the back of the room. 'Then your life will be so boring, you'll never need self-control.' Nearly everyone laughed except Charlie, who was looking at his feet as if he was wishing he could be somewhere else.

Nick Lightfinger's lips didn't even twitch. 'True. But let's try and think of something a bit less extreme. Anyone got any ideas? ... OK, I'll tell you how it's done. All you need to remember is this.'

He turned to the whiteboard and wrote:

Dull. Think only dull thoughts. Allow nothing stimulating into your brain and remember that excitement is your enemy.

Iceberg. Pretend you're an iceberg — cold, unthinking, deadly.

Movement. Restrict your movements to the absolute minimum necessary to achieve your goal. Move economically, like a leopard moving in for the kill.

Lightfinger turned back to the class. 'Thinking DIM will strongly enhance your chances of success in the field of forcible acquisition. Maybe you'll be nearly as successful as me. Eventually.' He smiled without opening his mouth, emphasising his puffy jowls even more. Now he looked like a hamster with full cheek pouches.

Milly gave Charlie a pained look. 'Think DIM! Is he for real?' she whispered. 'Do you think he ever uses the word "steal"?'

Seeing the dusty little teacher smirking and puffing out his chest, she added, 'Oh goody. He's ready to tell us his wonderful news. I can hardly wait.'

CHAPTER FIVE

S lightly pink with pride, Lightfinger was saying: 'I usually like to start new trainees off gently with a simple task involving bringing me the Great Clock of Blaggard before the end of the lesson. But today is different...'

Milly saw confusion on Charlie's face. 'It's a massive gold clock. In the Assembly Hall. Impossible to pinch, so I've heard. So it's not a fair challenge, no matter how much *self-control* you've got,' she whispered, throwing Lightfinger a dirty look.

'...I hope you realise how lucky you are. I'm introducing a new school competition – the Lightfinger Trophy. It's named after – well – me. Here it is.' He scurried behind his desk and pulled something out from behind it. He stood up and brandished a huge silver cup. 'I obtained it specially, from Messrs Glimmer and Glint, Jewellers to the Her Majesty the Queen. After closing hours, obviously!' He gave a modest smile.

'It'll be awarded to the team of Blaggardians who

demonstrate outstanding skill in unlawful redistribution. The competition is compulsory for all students. And I've thought up an excellent way of ensuring sure that everyone tries their hardest. Just take a little look at this rule sheet...'

He glided among the desks, handing out sheets of paper.

Milly scanned through it.

The Lightfinger Trophy
Just A Few Rules

· Only one entry per group – mix up the age groups. Brain + experience + muscle + enthusiasm = Success
· Your entry can't be a person or an animal. Animals bring me out in a nasty rash. And people, too, sometimes.
· No help from adults.
· Bring your entry to the Grand Submission Day.
· The most valuable entry wins.
· The team with the least valuable entry will be EXPELLED.

There was a collective gasp as the Year Sevens read the final bullet point. Watching Lightfinger as he tried not to smile, Milly's own lips thinned. *Creep! That's just not necessary. Or fair. I'm gonna say something.* She stuck up her hand. 'Sir, we haven't had a single Thievery lesson yet. The older years have had loads! How are we supposed to compete with them?'

'That's why I'm suggesting that you baby Blaggardians team up with the older years. You'd be very foolish not to. And you don't look foolish.' He peered at the name on Milly's pencil case.

'Milly Dillane – you're the daughter of Arthur and Dymphna Dillane? Well then – it'll be easy for you! Your parents are shining examples of shady success. Arthur Dillane is the most successful art forger in the world, and Dymphna's skills as a solver of criminal problems are legendary. No matter how dire your situation, Dymphna Dillane can make it go away.'

Milly was unconvinced and it showed on her face. Lightfinger quickly turned to Charlie and read his name. 'Aha, one of the kidnapping Partridges?' he said. 'I thought so – you're the spitting image of your father.'

Charlie's cheeks flamed and he ducked his head as Lightfinger continued.

'A few years ago, the Partridges were masters at the art of kidnapping. But then they seemed to lose their mojo. A few bungled jobs, a few lucky escapes from the law–' Lightfinger's face was a mixture of disapproval and sadness. 'And now I hear they've given up kidnapping completely and they're turning to new-fangled crime – computer hacking, identity theft – all those "safe" don't get your hands dirty things. Such a shame...' Lightfinger shook his head.

Seeing Charlie duck even lower, as if he was trying to hide behind his desk, Milly scowled at Lightfinger and turned to her new friend.

'Wow! You're a hacker!' she said, loudly. 'That's amazing. I'm rubbish at stuff like that. My Mum says that's where the future of criminality is. Not in all the old stuff like burgling and robbery...'

Charlie shot her a look of gratitude and sat up a bit.

When Charlie had recovered his composure, Milly asked, 'What happens to the entries when the competition ends, Sir?'

'You bring them to the Grand Submission, where they'll be valued by me and Ms Martinet. She's not *too* bad at loot assessment. Oh, and there'll be a special guest judge, too. Then they'll be sold off and the proceeds split between two excellent causes. Half will be donated to charity – Care for Old Wrongdoers, actually. I'm sure we all know some old crim who's dependent on COW now that their felonious days are behind them. Yes?'

Most of the class nodded.

'What about the other half?' Agatha Quint asked.

'It's going towards my retirement fund. It's not easy being this forgettable. Actually, it's exhausting. I may have to retire early. For health reasons.'

At last it was the end of the lesson and the class was packing up.

'So we're supposed to risk our necks to set Nick Lightfinger up in a beige bungalow by the sea. Not if I have anything to do with it,' Milly muttered to Charlie, not realising that Lightfinger had glided to a halt behind them.

The teacher's hamster cheeks were tinged red as he leant between them and said, 'There's nothing wrong with beige, Milly Dillane! And by all means *do* refuse to take part in the competition. The psychopaths at Crumley's

26

will be waiting to welcome you with open arms. I strongly suspect that you won't be much of a loss to Blaggard's.'

-oOo-

Milly and Charlie left Thievery deep in thought and drifted aimlessly for a few minutes. Eventually Milly voiced what was on her mind. 'I'm surprised you don't know more about Blaggard's – you know, the possible ambushes and the Great Clock and stuff. Your parents were Blaggardians, too, weren't they? Didn't they tell you what to expect?'

'Not really,' Charlie said, with a rueful smile. 'They're nearly always away on some criminal course or other, trying to work out what to do instead of kidnapping. They've decided that hacking is their best bet but they're not very good at it. I *am* quite good, so they're piling all their expectation onto me...'

Milly felt a surge of sympathy for her new friend. 'Oh well. When you're the world's top tyrant, sitting in your gigantic glass house on your own island and wondering what to do with all your riches, you'll thank them, probably.'

'Yeah, maybe.' Charlie stopped and looked around. 'We should be in Fabrication. I wonder where the classroom is? All these corridors look the same. Can't you remember from the map in the prospectus?' he asked.

Milly shrugged. 'Sorry, I must have missed Fabrication when I was memorising it. If William Proctor's right there'll be a painting on the door. So how do you paint Fabrication?'

'The next two doors *both* show computers,' Charlie said, examining them. 'One's being used by kid who looks totally confused. On the other there's a smirking boy

27

who probably gets beaten up a lot. Nothing to do with Fabrication – Hacking, I reckon.'

As they rounded a corner, they had to push through a giggling crowd of older pupils fresh out of a Disguise lesson. Milly and Charlie struggled past an elderly lady with a sharp pair of knitting needles, a police inspector with a droopy moustache and a six-foot baby in a romper suit.

Finally, at the far end of yet another corridor they came across a door painted with a blushing girl holding her hands over her mouth.

'This must be Fabrication. Although a good liar wouldn't look so embarrassed. It'd give her away. Here goes,' Milly commented. She pushed at the door.

CHAPTER SIX

The Fabrication teacher, a sweaty man with blue eyes, a wide forehead and clusters of dark curls, was fussily laying equipment on each desk.

'Just in time!' His voice was a high-pitched whine. 'I'm glad you managed to find me. I *still* can't believe they moved me down here! I'm Edgar Borgia. Find a seat. And don't touch the equipment yet.'

Milly and Charlie found empty desks and looked around, perplexed. The classroom was neat and bright and – odd. The walls were lined with thick plastic padding that had been fashioned into little mounds. It looked as if someone had stapled a whole load of blue egg boxes onto the walls.

'It's soundproofing. Ms Martinet insisted. The other teachers were complaining. It's jealousy, of course,' Borgia continued.

He closed the door, cutting off all sound of the outside world.

Lying on every desk was a metal headband attached to a long piece of plastic-coated wire. The wire plugged into a piece of machinery the size of a cornflake packet, with a pair of alarm bells attached to the top. There was one machine for each Blaggardian. Set into these devices was a semi-circular display board, marked *TRUE* and *LIE*. A thin red needle was fastened between the words. Protruding from each contraption were two thinner wires, ending in soft suction cups. The Year Sevens peered at them and then at each other.

Beneath a jumper that looked like it had been knitted by his granny, Borgia's chest swelled with pride. 'They're Truth Detectors,' he said. 'I invented them. They detect when you're *not* lying. They're highly sensitive. In a while we're all going to link up to them, me included, so you can see a professional Fabricator at work. From then on, everything you say must be an artificial truth. We're going to fire questions at each other to try and catch each other out. You'll find it quite hard to begin with, but you'll get the knack in the end. Everyone ready?'

Borgia went around each desk, explaining how to adjust the headbands and how the plastic suckers attached to the wrists, over the pulse. 'OK? I'll start. You join in when you're ready. No hesitating. If you hesitate, everyone will know you're lying. Stay sharp. Get those brain cells buzzing. Here goes.'

He looked quickly into Agatha Quint's eyes. 'You. What do you want to be when you grow up?'

Agatha hesitated for a second. The needle on her truth detector began swinging to the left, towards the word TRUE. 'A brain surgeon,' she spluttered, before the needle hit the word. It swung sharply back and came to rest on the word 'LIE'.

'Good, but you need to be faster. And you were tempted to tell the truth for a second, weren't you? You've got to stamp that out. Truth is your enemy.' He swung around to William Proctor. 'What's your favourite meal?'

'Beans on toast,' William replied, without blinking.

'Good! You – what do your parents or guardians do for a living?' Borgia was looking straight at Charlie, who'd picked up the truth detector from his desk and was inspecting it.

Milly saw surprise in Charlie's face. He opened his mouth. The needle on the machine on his desk was already swinging towards TRUE.

'They're kidnappers,' he said, as if he couldn't help himself. And then he added, 'Oh, squirrox!'

The needle hit TRUE and stayed there, juddering slightly. The alarm on his detector began to shrill. At the same time, blue and green lights, fastened into the corners of the room, flashed on and off, on and off.

'Loser,' someone muttered behind him.

Milly winced. Her new friend obviously had trouble with some of the basic precepts of criminality. Her heart gave a sympathetic twist. She knew how that felt. Time to rescue him. She gave him a look full of admiration.

'Charlie – you're a genius,' she breathed. 'You've beaten the Truth Detector!'

'Eh?' Charlie was looking confused.

'Well, they're not kidnappers any more, are they? But the Truth Detector didn't pick that up!' Milly looked around at the other Year Sevens. 'Charlie's worked out a way of beating it – tell it something that used to be true but isn't any more!'

The Year Sevens gave a short round of applause. Edgar Borgia looked a little put out, but he joined in after a few second's hesitation.

'Thanks,' Charlie muttered to Milly. 'I was gonna say that they ran a hotel. That would have been *almost* true. It's just that their guests were a bit reluctant.'

Milly gave him a little wink. 'No problem,' she said. 'So, have you got a pet?'

'Eh? Oh, yes,' Charlie said. 'An iguana. It's called Mavis.' The truth detector swung towards LIE, twice in succession. 'What do you want to be when you grow up?' Charlie threw back at her, looking happier by the second.

'A ballerina.' Milly's green eyes danced as Charlie snorted with laughter. 'How about you?'

'I want to breed stunt bats for vampire movies,' Charlie Fabricated happily.

They stopped for a moment to listen to William Proctor assuring his interrogators that his favourite colour was vomit yellow, his mother was a florist and he'd never EVER told a lie in his entire life.

Eventually, everyone had enough of Fabricating so they began telling the truth, for the fun of the setting off the alarms. Soon the windows were shaking with a dozen simultaneous trills. The soundproofing muffled the racket quite effectively, but to anyone standing outside and seeing the constantly flashing lights, it would have seemed that there was a silent disco in progress.

When Borgia realised what was happening, he huffed

and switched off the power supply. 'I don't think you're taking this seriously,' he moaned. 'We'll move on to the next part of the lesson. When I turn the power back on, I'll connect myself to the truth detector. It's *your* job to try and catch me out in a non-fabrication. It won't be easy. Ready?'

This was too good an opportunity to miss. The questions flew thick and fast. And so did Borgia's answers. 'Yes, I *love* animals. My favourite? Dormice. No, I never eat meat. I'm a fruitarian. Where did I go to school? I was home-schooled after I was eight. Why? Because I developed a phobia for teachers after one tried to get me to make a nightie in a needlework class.' He was perfectly at ease, lounging back behind his desk and studying his nails.

'He's pretty good,' Charlie said, in an undertone. 'Think we can fluster him?'

'Let's give it a go,' Milly said, with a sparkle in her eyes. She thought for a second and then threw a question at Borgia. 'Why's lying important?'

Borgia stretched and folded his arms behind his head. 'It's not important, obviously.' The red needle on his truth detector swung to LIE.

'If it's not important, why teach it?' Charlie joined in.

'Because – because – actually it's...' the red needle was swinging towards TRUE '– because I enjoy teaching unimportant things!' Borgia managed, sitting up. The needle swung back to LIE but it stayed there only a second before returning to its central position. It was a pretty lame answer.

Agatha Quint gave Milly and Charlie a look of grudging admiration. 'So Fabrication's a waste of time?' she asked.

'Yes!' The needle leapt to LIE.

Milly scented victory and quickly took over the questioning again. 'So you wouldn't mind if we told Ms Martinet that you think Fabrication's a waste of everyone's time?'

'YES! I mean No! I mean – *oh dear* ...' it was too late. The red needle dashed to TRUE and stayed there. The alarm blared and all around the room, peacock-coloured lights strobed.

Borgia tottered to his feet and switched off the power supply. 'The lesson's finishing early today. I need to lie down,' he faltered, wiping his forehead with a limp-looking hanky.

Most of the Year Sevens cheered and dashed through the door before he could change his mind. Agatha was one of the last, and she gave Milly a look of resentment as she passed, leaning close to a friend and whispering something into his ear. Milly gave her a wide smile and turned to close the door on the traumatised teacher.

CHAPTER SEVEN

I t was the end of the school day, and Milly and Charlie were longing for some time to think. But there was something they had to do first; it was finally time to settle into their new bedrooms. Mrs Christie, the head of boarding, was waiting for the Year Sevens on the first floor. She was wearing a flowery overall that reminded Milly of a granny's tablecloth. It gaped over her generous chest.

'You've got a bit of time now to make yourselves at home,' she said in a wheezy voice. 'I'm sorry it's so late in the day but your luggage has to go through strict security checks before we release it to you. There's always a newbie or two who thinks they'll get away with smuggling in something naughty.'

She shook her head and gave an indulgent smile. 'I'll name no names, but a pair of handcuffs that give *nasty* electric shocks have been confiscated. Also a well-cuddled teddy bear.' Looking at her companions, Milly saw that Agatha Quint and William Proctor were staring fixedly at the floor.

The boarding mistress ignored them. 'You're lucky, you know, dears: if your parents had been mad enough to send you to Crumley's you'd be locked into giant dorms at night. I don't like to even think about what would've happened to you by morning. Here, the bedrooms don't even have locks. There'd be no point. Pretty soon, you'll be able to pick any lock you fancy... Come here, dears, and look through these windows.'

She pointed into the distance, where a building could just be seen on the top of a steep hill. Milly saw a prison out of a nightmare – all spikes and spindly towers. '*That's* Crumley's School for Career Criminals,' Mrs Christie said, with a shudder. 'They say that Crumley's was actually built in a little valley, hundreds of years ago. But they bury all the Crumleians who die there in the school grounds, and over the centuries, that hill has formed from their bodies.' Her eyes were full of horror as she added: 'It won't be long before it's a *mountain.*'

Then she seemed to pull herself together. She indicated a poster attached to the door that led to the bedrooms. 'There are a few simple rules we ask you to follow as you decorate your rooms – they're laid out here, and there are copies in every bedroom. Be good trainee tyrants and stick to them. I'll be making an inspection before dinner to check.'

DECORATING YOUR ROOM:
HELPFUL HINTS

<u>DO</u> make sure that your posters, photos, postcards, etc don't offend others. Many Blaggardians are sensitive and easily upset by Dependable artwork. As long as your wall decorations have a strong criminal element but are reasonably free of gore (the boarding mistress is squeamish), you'll be fine.

<u>DON'T</u> expect to get away with posters, photos, etc of distasteful Dependable subjects. These include (but are not limited to):

* Paintings/drawings/photos of cute animals, ESPECIALLY when they are accompanied by inspirational sayings concerning, for instance:
    * Friendship
    * Honesty
    * Love.

(NB: Dependable sayings are not acceptable even if they do not accompany a picture of a cute animal. Or even an ugly one.)

* Paintings/Drawings/Photos of flowers and pretty landscapes UNLESS:
    * You can prove that the plants are dangerous and you're considering using them in a future crime.
    * The landscape is a crime scene, in which case it MUST contain some kind of reference to that crime, i.e. piles of swag in front of picturesque cottage, etc, etc.
* We STRONGLY discourage family and pet pictures of any kind – even extended family. Blaggard's is a school for trainee tyrants, and tyrants are loners. Get used to it.
* NB: Posters of inspirational criminals, e.g. Thomas Blaggard, Griselda Martinet, Pecunia Badpenny, etc, etc, are positively ENCOURAGED.

Milly and Charlie read the instructions with disbelief. 'More rules. I had enough of those at home.' Charlie grouched. 'I don't think I've got a single picture that's not "unsuitable". And as for posters of Pecunia Badpenny – have you *seen* her?'

Milly raised her eyebrows. 'I know my parents went to school with her and they hated her. The feeling was mutual. She's ultra successful, though – she's always boasting about her exploits on Crimbook. I suppose that's what makes her a suitable poster girl.' She hesitated and then continued: 'What's your house like? It doesn't sound very – homely?'

Charlie shrugged. 'Big. Very clean. Full of books that no one ever reads and art that no one looks at, except me. All chosen because it creates the right impression. It's really quiet, too. Everything's up to date and perfect. A muddy shoe is a crime in our house!' He thinned his lips. 'Anyway, how about you? What's your house like?'

'Hidden,' Milly said. 'Our real home's hidden beneath a tatty bungalow. There are even gnomes and goldfish in the garden! You go through a secret entrance and then down in a lift. Once you're in our *real* home, it's comfortable. Usually it smells of oil paint and cooking. Or burning, if Dad's making dinner. And it's quite noisy, especially when Dad's having one of his fits of artistic inspiration.'

Milly looked at Charlie's downcast eyes. She gave him a little shove. 'Anyway, this is a chance to practise our Fabrication skills. I think I can use these stupid guidelines to persuade Mrs Christie that my posters are suitable! And if I can do it, you can too.'

An hour later, Mrs Christie knocked on the door of Room 27, and entered to find Milly plumping up some rainbow-coloured cushions. She'd dumped her new schoolbooks on the floor, although her sketchbook and coloured pencils were neatly aligned on her little desk. She had opened her window to let in some air. Her view was of Blaggard's woods and beyond them, the cosy rooftops of the sleepy town of Borage Bagpuize. Charlie was lounging against one of the walls. 'He's here to borrow some drawing pins,' Milly explained.

Mrs Christie peered around at the posters that now covered the walls. There was a painting of an old ship on a sun-dappled sea, several of strong-jawed knights rescuing maidens or skewering dragons and a strange picture of three blue people with one eye and twelve arms between them.

The boarding mistress closed the door behind her, folded her arms over her ample bosom and shook her head. 'They're very pleasant, dear, but I'm afraid there's not a hint of criminality in them. You'll have to take them all down and replace them with something more suitable. Some nice "Wanted" posters, perhaps? There's a *lovely* one of the Blameless Family in this month's Racketeers' Review – posing on a beach.'

Milly looked up at Mrs Christie. She took care not to catch Charlie's eye. 'You don't need to worry, Miss. They're all fakes by my dad. He's a forger, quite an infamous one. See this poster with the ship? That's in the International Gallery. And the one with the girl drooping out of the tower? That's in the collection of a famous singer – he paid a *fortune* for it.

'Anyway, I reckon she's about to jump off the tower, because she's fed up with dim knights trying to rescue her. Maybe she likes it up there!' As Milly warmed to her theme, her eyes began to sparkle. 'She'll aim for that knight who's climbing it – how do you climb a tower in armour, anyway? He'll fall with her and they'll end up in a puddle of blood. So it's actually a picture of a crime in the making. When I look at these pictures, I think about what a brilliant forger my dad is. It makes me want to be as successful as he is.'

The boarding mistress beamed. 'Of course, dear. I've heard of your father – he's a *lovely* forger, I've been told. Just make sure that you don't allow any non-forgeries to slip in. Or anything sentimental. Carry on!' She gave a nod of approval and left.

Milly touched the poster of the three blue people. It was a portrait of her family, painted by her father in a Picasso mood, and it broke several of Mrs Christie's rules. But no one would ever know.

Milly considered her parents. Elegant Dymphna who'd never been known to lose her cool or look as if she hadn't just stepped out of a beauty salon. And Arthur, permanently spattered in paint and incapable of finding so much as a pair of socks that matched. Both were completely dedicated to criminal life and they never had any doubts about what they were doing. Milly wondered if she would ever feel the same certainty.

She found a grin and turned to Charlie. 'You're up next. I reckon you've got half an hour to get your story straight.'

40

CHAPTER EIGHT

Charlie was back in his room on the second floor – the one above Milly's. The first thing he did was close his curtains. When they were open, there was nothing to block his view of Crumley's School for Career Criminals. Lurking on its sinister hill, it seemed to be beckoning him. Or threatening him.

Then he plugged in his laptop and set up his homemade web booster. Blaggard's bedrooms were meant to be Internet black spots, for safety reasons, but Charlie wasn't going to let that stop him. It didn't take him long to establish a strong connection. He tucked the booster under his bed, out of sight and then got to work on his walls.

In ten minutes flat he'd plastered the walls with pages from magazines featuring interviews with techno-pioneers and influential hackers (who liked to be photographed wearing balaclavas or with bandanas over their noses) and close-up photos of what looked like bits of metallic Lego. In between these were photos of Gruffles – a grubby cloud leaping into puddles and rolling in sludge.

There was a knock at the door. Mrs Christie came in, inspected his walls, pursed her lips and shook her head. 'They'll have to come down, dear. They're just not criminal. Why don't you pop along to William Proctor's room, for some inspiration? He's made it into a shrine to Sir Thomas Blaggard.'

Charlie had been preparing himself and now he unleashed his best villainous look on her. It consisted of narrowed eyes and a sinister curl of the lips. He'd spent hours over the summer holidays practicing it. He'd based it on Gavin McGlintock, the coolest expert on his favourite criminal TV show, *The Robbery Roadshow*, in which thieves brought things they'd pinched to menacing mansions in the dead of night to be valued by experts in stocking masks.

Gavin McGlintock didn't bother with a mask. He was greyhound thin, with oiled back hair and an unexpectedly charming smile, which he didn't use much. His nickname was the *Sneering Specialist* and viewers waited for his catchphrase – *'Sorry, it's not worth the wear on your crowbar'* – with bated breath. Every week it reduced some hard-bitten criminal to a snivelling wreck.

Charlie gave the boarding mistress a look of pity. 'I can understand your confusion, but actually they're totally unDependable. The computer stuff gives me loads of ideas on how to improve my hacking skills. And these hackers are all top criminals – really infamous in their field.'

'Well, I *suppose* that's acceptable, as long as they're not relatives. But what about these doggy photos? He looks suspiciously like a family pet.' Mrs Christie was peering at the photos of Gruffles as she would at a nasty stain that she'd found on her overall.

Charlie had prepared for this, too. The portrait of Sir Bryon de Bohun's massive dog had given him an idea. 'That's Gruffles. He pretends to be my pet, but I'm training him as a merciless attack beast. I don't call him a dog. Dogs can be cute and cuddly. To call Gruffles a dog is like calling Godzilla a newt. His name was chosen to disguise his real personality. If I'd called him Fang, he wouldn't be able to surprise anyone.'

Mrs Christie considered him. Then she examined the photos again. Eventually she said: 'Well, dear, you must be a *wonderful* trainer of evil animals. He looks utterly gormless to me. And I don't fool easily!'

Charlie struggled to keep his face straight.

When she'd gone, Charlie made a mental note to thank Milly. *She's great – clever and kind of brave, too. I wonder if there's a chance she's like me? I'll have to find out.*

He thought through the day's events. What bugged him most was Nick Lightfinger – his smug self-regard and his stupid competition that might well end Charlie's own time at Blaggard's almost before it had started. And then he'd be chucked into the wolf lair that was Crumley's. *Lightfinger's so pleased with his iceberg 'self-control'. I wonder if he ever loses it? Says or does something he'll regret later? Maybe I'll give him a hand...*

It took him only a minute or two to hack into Nick Lightfinger's emails. *His security's rubbish – no challenge at all!* He sent Ms Martinet a message on the Thievery teacher's behalf:

43

Dear Griselda, I hope you don't mind me
calling you by your first name? I look
on you as an equal and I'm sure you
feel the same.

I've got two reasons for writing to
you. The first is related to money. I'm
clearly the best teacher at Blaggard's.
You know it and I know it. So – how
about a pay rise? I really think I
deserve one. A big one. The sooner, the
better, please.

The second reason is this. We both know
that you're not getting any younger and
that thoughts of your successor must be
uppermost in your head. I wonder if we
can meet up sometime soon for a cup of
tea and the chance to talk about it? It
takes time to train a good successor
and the sooner we start, the better.

Love Nick. xxx

Charlie grinned as he hit SEND. The bit about wanting
Ms Martinet's job was especially good, he thought.

Then he accessed the little camera he'd set up at home,
over Gruffles' bed. The dog was on its side, twitching in its
sleep. Charlie decided that his pet was dreaming about cats
or rabbits. He seemed to be determined to rid the world of
both of these dangerous species.

In the background he saw his mum's feet, encased in

feathery white slippers. She began dragging a bath towards the dog. Gruffles half-opened one eye, saw the bath, leapt to his paws and bolted. *Poor Gruffles. Hope he's OK. One day he'll have enough of all that bathing.* There was nothing he could do to help his dog, so Charlie alternated between playing a video game and checking out the outrageous boasts on Crimbook, while he waited for dinner.

CHAPTER NINE

At 6.30, the shimmering *CRASH* of a gong echoed through Blaggard's. Milly wasn't the only Year Seven to leave her room with a mixture of excitement and misgiving. She'd heard sensational stories about the food fights at Blaggard's and, while they sounded like fun, she didn't feel that their first day was the ideal time to experience one. *I wouldn't want to cover someone in custard and then find out they're the school kick boxing champion!*

The Dining Room was huge – the size of four tennis courts joined together – and very modern. The long, white tables were already crammed with chatting diners. Around the walls, below the high windows, there were flashing digital signs.

'NO FOOD FIGHTS! THIS MEANS YOU, HARRY BLACKMORE. SHADY MANNINGTON. NATASHA ARKADY.'

The names changed frequently. Milly peered around. *Weird! Who was monitoring the crowd?*

The food was served from polished steel counters at one end of the room. Overhead was the biggest sign of all.

NUMBER OF DAYS SINCE LAST FOOD FIGHT: 2.

Milly noted the green and yellow splotches on the sign and raised one eyebrow.

As Milly watched, an older Blaggardian made a grab for a jug of gravy. Someone, somewhere, spotted the manoeuvre. A siren shrieked. Immediately, pitted glass screens sprang up in front of the counters, protecting the servers and preventing further food snatches.

Griselda Martinet had been standing nearby, choosing her meal. In less than a second she was on the case, seizing the jug and saying something to the thief that made him blench and stagger away, to the cheers and jeers of the other Blaggardians. A few seconds later the digital signs were displaying a new message:

RODERICK MACDUFF – YOU ARE EXPECTED IN MS MARTINET'S OFFICE AT 4PM. BRING A BOX OF TISSUES.

The newbies found Edgar Borgia waiting for them with a clipboard. 'Are all the Year Sevens here?' He was counting them as he spoke. 'Ms Martinet has told me to show you the ropes. I don't have long. I need to go and arrange a very dastardly crime....'

Milly threw the teacher a sharp look. *I'm pretty sure he's Fabricating.*

Borgia escorted the Year Sevens past the seated older

year groups, who assessed them all with narrowed eyes. One boy caught Milly's attention. He looked to be about 15 with a powerful frame and hair so black it just *had* to be dyed. His face was round and it was marred by a sneer. '... and I bought a new designer burglar's mask, from Cloak and Dagger's online shop,' he was saying in a voice that seemed to belong to a younger boy. 'It was a one-off. It's got silver skulls hanging from the ties. It cost – well, more than most of you could afford...'

When the newbies passed by, the boy nudged those sitting next to him. 'We'll see you later, little babies,' he said.

That might sound threatening if his voice was lower, Milly thought. 'Not if we see you first,' she retorted. There was a ripple of amusement on the boy's table.

Borgia showed them to a rectangular table, a long way from the serveries. Enticing aromas followed them. There was no limp lettuce or shrivelled hot dogs at Blaggard's. Instead Blaggardians enjoyed a choice of fresh pasta, juicy steaks and homemade chicken nuggets the size of baked potatoes.

Milly focused on Edgar Borgia's high voice. 'As you progress through the school you get closer and closer to the serving counters. I suppose it's a bit harsh on the younger students, but if you want fair, go and join the Dependables at Borage Bagpuize High School. By the way, did I tell you about the time I found a gold ring in my school spag bol? With a mouldy finger still attached?'

Several Year Sevens turned away to gag, but Milly wasn't fooled. *That's definitely a lie. And not even a very good one.*

'It's OK. Remember, he teaches Fabrication,' she murmured, as Borgia walked away.

When they'd filled their plates, the new Blaggardians settled around their table and compared notes.

'I must say I'm extremely pleased. Blaggard's is going to be everything it promised to be,' said William Proctor, who seemed to be able to eat steak and fat chips, chat and read a book on Advanced Manipulation, all at the same time.

'Didn't your parents come here? I thought that was the only way of getting in.' Charlie looked up from the game he was playing on his mobile, and regarded Proctor with interest.

'They went to... another establishment for the education of criminals to be. I persuaded them that Blaggard's was more likely to offer the type of course I need to achieve my ambitions, and I applied for a scholarship,' William said, in a manner that seemed a bit defensive.

'They went to *Crumley's*? I've never met a Crumleian before. Does Ms Martinet know? Is it as horrific as people say?' This was a sleepy-eyed girl called Sophie, who'd just revealed that her ambition was to be a blackmailer. She leaned across the table as she spoke, poking a fork loaded with pasta towards him.

'Well,' Proctor seemed to be struggling to find the right words. 'I hesitate to say anything negative about the school that shaped both my parents. They survived intact. Mainly. It didn't take my father long to get used to his electronic hand. In fact, he says it's a blessing. Much stronger than his real one.' He gave an uncertain smile. 'He finds it really useful for the more physical aspects of his work.

49

He doesn't need to hire muscly stooges any more. There's more strength in his electric hand than in half a dozen of them! And Mother says she's finally learning to control her nightmares...'

The other Year Sevens exchanged uncertain glances. 'Great,' Milly said, eventually, to fill the silence. 'What was the scholarship? Was it the TAWDRY?'

Charlie frowned. 'What's the TAWDRY?' He flushed at the look of surprise on Proctor's face. 'My mum and dad are really busy,' he continued, quickly. 'They meant to tell me about it, I'm sure. They just forgot.'

'It's for Tyrants Aiming for World Domination Really Young,' Proctor explained. 'The exam was extremely tough. It lasted for ten hours! I had to give detailed plans for taking over an entire continent, starting with a village, then working up to a town, then a city, then a country and so on. Fortunately I've been thinking of little else since I organised a rebellion at my nursery when I was three, when they tried to phase out our break-time milk.'

Milly tried to think of something to say. 'Wow! That's fantastic,' she managed. 'Anyway, I'm off to my room. Night everyone.' She stood up to leave.

-oOo-

It was late that night and Blaggard's was relatively peaceful. Lying in her bed, Milly listened to the unfamiliar sounds of the building settling down. The creaks of ancient woodwork were offset by whirs and clicks, as the school's high-tech security system ensured the safety of those who were sleeping inside it, or at least trying to sleep. A sudden strangled beep made Milly frown. *It sounds like the security's been switched off*, she thought.

Alert now, she sat up. Other sounds reached her. A slow c-r-e-a-k, as if someone was trying to open a door undetected. The almost-silent pad of many footsteps. A snigger, hastily cut short. Before Milly could react, her door was snatched open. All along the corridor, she heard cries of surprise from people being shaken awake. A hand punched on Milly's light switch. Blinking in the sudden harsh light, Milly saw two older Blaggardians, grinning at her.

'Get your dressing gown. You're coming with us,' one of them said.

CHAPTER TEN

Milly's captors shoved her into the corridor, where she joined the other Year Sevens who were being shepherded onto the landing. When the newbies with rooms on the second floor had joined them, they were all manhandled downstairs. She fought her way over to Charlie. He was wearing a black, hooded dressing gown and his hair was wilder than ever.

Milly rolled her eyes. 'Some sort of dumb initiation ceremony, I reckon,' she said.

'The perfect end to the perfect day,' Charlie replied, with a twist of his lips.

Downstairs, the rest of the school was waiting for them. A heavy boy with prominent ears stepped forward.

'Baby Blaggardians, for many years it has been traditional for newbies to end their first day with an encounter with a very special member of the school. Yes, it's time to meet Pickpocket Pete!' he declared.

Their captors cheered wildly. The older students grabbed

the Year Sevens by their arms and hustled them past the marble desk in Reception and through a heavy door.

Milly peered around. They were in a huge, dim room that looked as if it didn't see much use. It contained stacks of old wooden desks with neat piles of cellophane-wrapped burglars' tops stacked on them. In one corner there lurked a set of ancient stocks, still spattered with the dried remains of eggs and nameless brown lumps. The ceiling was high and raftered. Long skeins of cobwebs drifted from it in a chilly draft.

A figure was standing in one corner. The dimness made it impossible to tell whether it was male or female. It had its back to them and it was swathed in a wide-brimmed hat and heavy overcoat. The strange person stood eerily still. *It's almost like he's disconnected his mind from his body and only the body's standing here,* Milly mused.

The heavy boy spoke again. 'Pickpocket Pete is the world's best pickpocket. He won't turn round or acknowledge you in any way – he's completely focused on his task. You see, Pete is a master of the ancient art of sense sharpening – it's called Yuh-Ah-Gul-La-Bul.

'Masters of Yuh-Ah-Gul-La-Bul are completely sensitive to the world around them. They can hear the beat of a butterfly's wings, or the way a mouse's heart flutters when it senses a nearby cat. They can detect the moment that a target starts to suspect that his pocket is being picked.'

Milly folded her arms. Her eyebrows rose into her fringe.

The boy hadn't finished yet. 'At this time of year, Pete feels that it's his duty to challenge the baby Blaggardians. He bets you can't pick his pocket without him feeling it.

If he catches you out, you pay a forfeit. If you beat him, there's treats for the whole school.'

'We're not falling for that,' Milly muttered. 'They call us babies, but we're not Crumleians.' But in front of them they could see other Year Sevens nodding.

'I reckon I'd be pretty good at Yuh-Ah-Gul-La-Bul,' said an eager boy with a wide smile and glasses. 'I'm Dylan Maguire. My family are the best smash and grabbers in the country. I'll go first!' He started forward, but Milly put out a hand to restrain him.

'Whoa, Dylan. Let's find out a bit more first.' She turned to the heavy boy. 'What are the rules and what's the forfeit?' she asked.

'The rules are simple. Pickpocket Pete remains exactly where he is. We'll cover his eyes so he can't see anyone approaching. He'll wear earplugs too. All he has to rely on is his super-sense. All *you* babies have to do is remove the object from his coat pocket without him sensing you. If he does feel you, he'll press that remote control he's holding. Then the unsuccessful pickpocket pays the forfeit.'

'The forfeit being...?' enquired William Proctor, suspiciously.

The boy assumed a look of innocence. 'That's a secret. Let's just say it's nothing that your parents wouldn't approve of.'

The Year Sevens stared at each other for a long moment.

It was the enthusiastic Dylan who broke the silence: 'OK. That sounds fine to me. I'm ready to go!'

'Hang on. We just need to help Pete get into the zone,' the heavy boy said.

It took a whole group of people to prepare Pete. He was completely still as someone removed his hat to tie his blindfold at the back of his head. A tall girl seemed to be having difficulty keeping a straight face as she fiddled with Pete's ears. Others just crowded around, grinning at each other.

As they turned back to join the others, the tall girl glanced upwards. Milly caught the glance and peered in the same direction, but she could see nothing except the shadowy roof and rafters. Dylan limbered up, shaking his arms and hopping from foot to foot.

Everyone was expecting Dylan to throw himself straight into the task. Instead, he removed his shoes and spent a long time assessing his target. Then he started to creep towards him.

There was absolute silence in the room as the spectators watched him stop dead for what seemed like ages, then start forward again. He repeated his actions several times. At last he was within touching distance of Pete.

Dylan's eyes roamed over Pete's coat. Eventually one of his hands edged forward, achingly slowly. When his fingers made contact with Pete's coat, just above one of the side pockets, they looked as gentle as butterflies landing on a flower.

Everyone held their breath.

CHAPTER ELEVEN

In the same instant a red light flashed in Pete's right hand.

Dylan peered around, looking for some clue about what was going to happen. Then an avalanche of water and ice cubes tumbled from the ceiling, drenching him. He gasped and jumped, sending his glasses flying. All the spectators except the Year Sevens exploded into laughter.

'I told you your parents would approve,' the heavy boy crowed. 'I bet they're always telling you to wash more often! Pete – One, Babies – Nil. You can give up any time you want. No one's ever beaten Pickpocket Pete.'

Dylan shook himself like a wet dog. He picked up his glasses and took a towel from Mrs Christie, who'd appeared with a tall pile of them and a sympathetic smile on her broad face. Milly activated the torch on her mobile phone and aimed it at the ceiling. There was a bucket swinging at the end of a rope. It was lowered to the floor and a pair of girls refilled it from a big bowl.

At the side of the room, the boy from the dining room

was lounging by himself against a wall. He was still sneering. *I think his face must be stuck like that,* Milly thought. She watched the boy straighten up lazily and hoist the bucket back to the ceiling.

William Proctor huffed. 'I'm assuming you have a conspirator up there who waits for someone to approach Pete and then shoves the bucket over? Some challenge. Don't expect any more "volunteers".'

'There's no one up there. You can check. The water won't drop until Pete presses the button,' the heavy boy said.

'What's to stop Pete just pressing the button anyway? He knows that someone must be close by,' said Charlie.

'Pete never lies. Although he tries, obviously.' As he spoke, the heavy boy peered past William. A tiny, slender girl seemed to appear out of nowhere. *Haven't noticed her before,* Milly thought.

'I'm Susie. I can do this,' the girl said in a voice that was so gentle, Milly had to lean close to hear her.

Susie approached Pete without hesitation, slipping into the shadows and aiming for the opposite pocket to the one Dylan had chosen. Milly held her breath. She realised that everyone was doing the same, straining their ears for the slightest noise from the tiny girl. The hand that Susie extended was as insubstantial as air, but the moment it touched Pete's coat, down came the freezing water.

Again and again it happened. Milly looked on as the group of shivering failures grew bigger. Each of the remaining Year Sevens became determined to be *the one* who rescued their group's honour. Everyone tried a different tactic. Some tried stealth. Or speed. Or distraction techniques, trying to jolt Pete out of his trance. Agatha Quint seemed to be aiming for a lightning attack, trying to slip her handcuffs over Pete's wrists before he could react. But in no time at all, she too was soaking and shuddering.

Milly spent a long time observing Pete. Then she started looking around the room. The boy in charge of hoisting the bucket was acting strangely. He stood in a dark corner, focused on Pete. If anyone stepped in front of him, he shoved them aside, none too gently. 'Something's not right here,' she whispered to Charlie. 'Look at Pete. No one can be that still for that long... I think he's a dummy.'

Charlie peered through the gloom at the frozen figure. 'I think you're right. But how can a dummy press a button? The red light comes on the second anyone touches him,' he murmured back.

'Look at the boy who pulls up the bucket. There's something in his hand. He's trying to hide it, but you can see it when he moves... There! It's a remote control. He presses it when someone touches Pete, and it makes the button in Pete's hand flash red and releases the lever holding up the bucket...'

Charlie was fiddling with his mobile. He held it up to show Milly. 'Look, I could use this app I've been working on. You aim it and it blocks signals from mobiles. I thought it could be useful for budding cyber criminals, like I'm supposed to be... I could use it to block the signal from Bucket Boy's handset...'

'While I get whatever's in Pete's pocket. Great! Ready? They've been making us look like monkeys for long enough.'

Charlie nodded. 'Yep. Let's get on with it.' He moved

away to stand opposite Bucket Boy. Casually, he pointed his mobile towards him.

Across the room, Milly gave Charlie a tiny wink. 'There aren't many of us left, so I suppose I might as well have a go,' she said, loudly. She marched straight up to Pete, not bothering to stifle the noise of her footsteps. She was humming tunelessly. The moment she extended her hand, Bucket Boy pressed his remote pad. Nothing happened. He frowned. Pressed it again. And again.

Milly took Pete by the shoulders and spun him around. His hat flew off, revealing the shiny head and rigid grin of a showroom dummy. Unhurriedly, she riffled in the dummy's coat pockets. 'Got it!' she called, brandishing a small flat package. As nearly all the Year Sevens cheered and clapped, she opened it. It was a plastic rain hat. She placed it on Pete's head and tied a sloppy bow beneath his chin. Then she grabbed Charlie and pulled him into the centre of the room, to join her in accepting the applause.

The older students were looking accusingly at Bucket Boy. It seemed that he'd completely forgotten about looking cool. He flushed. 'It's gone wrong. It's not my fault,' he exclaimed in his little boy's voice. He hurried towards the dummy, still pressing his remote.

Charlie threw Milly a mischievous smile. He waited until the boy had reached Pete and then switched off his app with a flick of his thumb. The light on Pete's device flashed and the bucket capsized, tipping its freezing contents over the older boy.

Everyone collapsed into shrieks of laughter.

'Nice one, Charlie!' Milly said.

Ms Martinet was smiling as she pushed through the crowd. 'Never mind, Jet. The babies were bound to work it out one day,' she said to the soaking, glaring boy. She turned to Milly and Charlie. 'The short girl with the attitude and the tall boy with the hair! Your names, please?'

Seeing Charlie blushing, Milly shoved him towards the Head Teacher. 'He's Charlie Partridge. I'm Milly Dillane.'

'Charlie. Milly,' Ms Martinet repeated. 'There'll be treats tomorrow to celebrate the first time that Pickpocket Pete's been beaten. Chocolate policemen for everyone!'

As he picked ice cubes out of his hair, Bucket Boy gave Milly a fake smile. When he was sure that no one was listening the grin slid away. 'You're going to regret that,' he whispered.

-oOo-

It was even later that night and Milly had given up trying to sleep. She was sitting up in bed, writing in her diary. She chewed on her pen for a bit and then wrote quickly. *Interesting day. Ms Martinet is WEIRD. I wonder if she's mixed up the letters of her name to disguise the fact she's really a Martian? Quite like her, though. Edgar Borgia – the Fabrication teacher – is a bit pathetic. Nick Lightfinger is a creeping idiot and as for his stupid competition – I just wish I could think of something disgusting to steal and slap into his hands on Presentation Day.*

She had a flash of inspiration and grabbed a pencil from the little table next to her bed. In just a few minutes she'd drawn Griselda Martinet as a sleek alien, a cowering mouse with Edgar Borgia's wide forehead and lank curls, and Nick Lightfinger trundling round in a hamster wheel, cheeks bulging. She smiled briefly at her doodles and then continued writing.

The Pickpocket Pete thing was fun in the end, but Bucket Boy will be after us now. Ms Martinet called him Jet. Seems fitting, somehow. So much for not making an enemy on Day One. I don't think Agatha Quint's my biggest fan, either. Oh well, I'll live.

I'm glad I've made friends with Charlie. He's cool – funny and clever at stuff that I'm useless at. I don't think he knows how clever he is! He's the opposite of me, then. I think I can do anything, if I feel like it. We should make a good team, especially as we seem to have a shared secret. He's not sure about being a hacker and I'm not sure about being a forger, or any other kind of felon, if it comes to it.

She frowned at her desk and then added: *He needs to harden up a bit, though, and try to act a bit more criminally. He makes his doubts obvious, and that's dangerous. I'll try and teach him to hide them.*

When she finished, she pulled a weighty book from a pile on the floor. Its title was so long that it didn't fit on the spine, running all the way down it before continuing onto the cover: '*Sir Bryon de Bohun – A Minutely Detailed Examination of His Life, Tragic Death and Legacy Over the Centuries (with numerous heart-warming anecdotes of his childhood from all twelve of his siblings and many of his friends and relations)*'. She flipped it open. It was hollow. She nestled the diary inside, and returned the book to its place in the pile.

'There you go,' she said to the diary. 'You're safer there

than in the deepest vault of the Bank of England. Unless William Proctor finds his way in here, looking for new reading material.'

CHAPTER TWELVE

Every morning started with an assembly, and after breakfast the next day Milly and Charlie joined the students streaming into the Assembly Hall for their first one.

Like all the rooms in Blaggard's, the hall belied the school's ancient exterior by being bright and modern, with room-high windows that let in long shafts of sunlight. The rays glinted on the Great Clock of Blaggard, a massive golden timepiece engraved with snarling bears and stinging nettles, Sir Thomas' emblems. The clock was secured to the wall by thick chains. It also had its own alarm system – a cage of thin beams of red light. Charlie touched Milly's shoulder and pointed to it. 'I see what you mean about it being impossible to pinch. Lightfinger's a total idiot,' he said.

At either side of the entrance, electronic handprint detectors were set into the walls. Every Blaggardian had to place a hand onto one of the screens to prove their identity and to register. Although the new intake hadn't been required to attend Assembly the previous day, William Proctor had explained the procedure before they entered the Hall.

When it came to his turn to register, Charlie examined them in detail. 'They're really cool! I bet I could modify them to say I'm here when I'm not,' he said.

After pulling him away, Milly and Charlie filed past rows of glass cabinets crammed with mementoes from Blaggard's history. They stopped to inspect Sir Thomas Blaggard's long johns with his favourite saying – *Cajole, Coerce, Control* – embroidered down the leg, and the champagne cork, encrusted with rusty blood, that had put a sudden end to Sir Bryon de Bohun's villainous career.

Charlie took a look and wrinkled his nose in disgust. Milly noticed and said, 'If you don't like those, make sure you don't look to your right.'

Automatically, Charlie looked right. He saw a waxwork dummy, sitting stiffly on a gilt chair in a glass cabinet. It was holding up a hand mirror that reflected the figure's expression of pained surprise. It was dressed in a flowery waistcoat, knee breeches and a yellowed shirt with a patch of what appeared to be dried ketchup over the heart.

Charlie laughed. 'Is it supposed to be Sir Bryon de Bohun? It's the worst waxwork I've ever seen. Why don't you want me to look at it?' He walked over and peered at it. 'It's rubbish! The eyes aren't even level. The wax must have melted. And his jaw's dropping off. Look – they've even put wax bones underneath the skin. You'd think they'd find it a clean shirt!'

Milly took his arm and steered him away before

replying. 'Well you're right about one thing. It's Sir Bryon de Bohun. He's been – taxidermed'.

Charlie looked confused. 'What's taxidermed? I'm guessing it's nothing to do with cars for hire? Or skin complaints?'

'You know what happens to turkeys at Christmas...' Milly began, carefully.

Charlie nodded. Then enlightenment hit him. His jaw dropped. 'You don't mean...? They *STUFFED* him?'

He wondered if he was imagining the ghoulish gleam in Milly's eyes. 'Yep. That *is* Sir Bryon. He left his body to the school. There used to be a taxidermy club here. Maybe it was one of their first attempts? They probably got better. And the shirt? It's the one he was wearing when he was killed.'

Charlie wrinkled his nose. 'That's *disgusting!*'

At that moment Ms Martinet stalked to the centre of a long stage at one end of the room. The rest of the teaching staff sat down behind her, with their backs to the wall. The Head Teacher glared as she passed Nick Lightfinger, and hesitated just long enough to slap a folded note into his hand. Lightfinger had been wearing his blandest smile, but as he opened the note and digested its contents, the smile congealed on his face. Charlie grinned. *She's read her email, then. I'd love to know what that note says!*

Griselda Martinet's gaze swept the room. 'Good morning, tyrants of tomorrow, and a special welcome to our new Year Sevens. We'll get straight to the topic of today's assembly. As you know, Blaggard's encourages healthy competition through its house system. It works well and results in very little violence. We've suffered a mere handful of fatalities in Blaggard's long history.

'For nearly two centuries there have been only two houses, one named after our beloved founder, Sir Thomas Blaggard, and the other after our illustrious student, Bryon de Bohun, whose life of crime was cut short by his wretched butler. I'll never believe that he "accidentally" aimed that champagne cork at Sir Bryon's heart!' She threw a regretful glance at the stuffed Sir Bryon.

'Recently, our numbers have risen dramatically, thanks to our unrivalled mastery at turning out successful scoundrels. Because of this, inter-house rivalry has reached unacceptable levels as students try to score a few points. I've therefore decided to change the system. I'm going add a new house to the current ones and start the points system again.'

There was a lot of muttering among the assembled Blaggardians. 'That's not fair!' a sturdy Indian boy called out.

Griselda Martinet's face was serene. 'There are several Dependable schools in the area if you're worried about fairness, Arnav Jai. I hear that the High School is offering a new course on "Citizenship",' She sketched the quotation marks in the air. 'They're bound to have student vacancies.'

The muttering stopped. There was an appalled silence.

'So,' the Head continued, smoothly. 'I'm asking you for suggestions about which member of the criminal community, alive or dead, should give their name to the new house. No Crumley's scumbags, please. There'll be tamper-proof ballot boxes in every classroom. You've got till next week to vote. That's it. I wish you all a villainous day.'

Ms Martinet leapt down from the stage with superb grace and left the hall, heralding a buzz of excited speculation.

'I'm voting for Mitch McTavish,' Charlie was eager to share his thoughts with Milly. 'Mum and Dad used to work with him. People pay him to kidnap them. When the ransom's paid, the person who was "kidnapped" splits it with Mitch McTavish. Then they change their name and disappear to Australia or Mongolia or somewhere. He calls it auto-napping. He's made a huge pile of money from it and he lives like a king. That's why his nickname's Lavish McTavish. He was always nice to me.'

Milly nodded. 'He sounds good. I'll tell you who I won't be voting for Pecunia Badpenny. I know she's famous and her Dial-a–Death service has made her a fortune. And she holds the world record for the number of victims blackmailed in a day, as she's always reminding everyone. But my dad reckons she's mad. And meaner than a whole class of Crumleians.

'When they were at Blaggard's, some bigger kids locked Dad in a classroom with Badpenny,' she continued after a moment. 'They were stuck there for hours. He won't tell me what she said, but by the time he got out his hair had gone white, and it's been white ever since! Blaggard's is tricky enough without her making it worse... Speaking of tricky situations, how are you feeling about Lightfinger's competition? Are you a good thief?'

Charlie's eyes slid away. 'Well... to be honest...'

'I thought so,' Milly leaned in close to Charlie. 'We've

got something in common, I think. I love art, but when it comes to forging or any other kind of criminal stuff I'm not that interested. As for stealing – you'd be better off asking Pickpocket Pete to go and pinch something.'

Charlie gave a slight nod. 'Same here. Computers are what grab me. And if it has to be criminal stuff, to keep my parents happy,' – he shrugged, '–I've got my doubts, but I'll try and give it a go. For their sake. But stealing? Gruffles is better at it than me. He's always raiding the biscuit tin.'

'Pity Gruffles couldn't come to Blaggard's, then!'

By this time, Milly and Charlie were jostling their way through the lines of Blaggardians leaving the Hall, comparing timetables as they went.

'They're nearly the same, but you're in Advanced Computer Hacking and I go to Hacking for the Useless. Nice. That explains the paintings on those classroom doors – I join the hopeless head-scratchers and you go with the brainboxes next door. How'd you get into Advanced Hacking?

Charlie gave a modest shrug. 'I'm not bad, actually. You know when you apply to join Blaggard's, you have to come and do some tests to prove you're good enough?'

'Yep, but that was basic stuff – a Fabrication test, and I had to follow a Sixth Former for five minutes without being detected. Nothing to do with Hacking.'

Charlie gave a sage nod. 'I mentioned in my application that my hobby was hacking. I suppose that was why they gave me an extra test. I had to hack into the Prime Minister's personal emails and insult her. I pretended I was a talent scout for a film company that was remaking *The Wizard of Oz* and I offered her a part.'

'What part?' Milly asked.

Charlie's lips twitched. 'Munchkin Warlord. The teacher said I might be the only decent hacker Blaggard's has ever produced.'

Milly struggled to control her giggles. 'It just proves what it says in the prospectus – there's villainy in all of us if you dig deep enough. There's hope for me yet. Lurking beneath my secret Dependable nature there might just be a throbbing pit of villainy!'

As the queue surged forwards, there was snigger behind them. Milly and Charlie turned to see Jet Mannington, so close he was virtually touching them. He gave them a knowing smile before peeling off towards the library.

'Don't worry,' Charlie said. 'He probably didn't hear anything.'

CHAPTER THIRTEEN

After Assembly, Milly and Charlie had their first Defiance and Discourtesy lesson.

They found the classroom without difficulty. Although it was among a cluster of other rooms, all branching off from a corridor decorated with a display of handcuffs and crowbars in symmetrical patterns, it was unmistakeable. On the door was a painting of a child blowing a raspberry. A sign above it said:

DON'T EVEN THINK ABOUT KNOCKING
BEFORE ENTERING!

Milly shrugged and shoved open the door. The classroom was deep red – the kind of red that was so oppressive, it gave her dad headaches. Even the bright rays of the sun seemed to run out of steam as they hit the windows. The walls were largely bare. Apart from a few form photos that looked as if they were clustering together for safety, the only thing to look at was a huge message, painted in thick black capitals and running all the way around the room:

RUDENESS IS A SKILL, NOT A GIFT. NO
MATTER HOW RUDE YOU ARE, YOU CAN BE
RUDER. YOU HAVE TO WORK AT IT. SO STOP
READING THIS MESSAGE AND CONCENTRATE!

Jane Vipond turned her neat head and glared. 'Finally. The last two Year Sevens. So pleased that you decided to join us. Sit down. Quickly.'

One look at the teacher had told Milly that Miss Vipond wasn't in the mood to be contradicted. *She probably never is!* But it seemed that Charlie hadn't noticed.

'Actually, Miss, we're not late. It's just that your clock's a bit fast,' Charlie said, double-checking the time on his waterproof, dog-proof mobile. Miss Vipond's eyebrows snapped together and she stomped over to him.

Ooh, nasty angle! I bet Charlie can see straight up her nose! Milly thought.

'Shut up,' the teacher snapped. 'You're interrupting me. And contradicting me. No one gets away with that!'

Charlie went pale and opened his mouth.

He's gonna apologise, Milly thought. *It'll be like waving a bulging bag of loot in front of a policeman. Got to do something!* Making sure that she wasn't speaking too quietly, she said: 'She's certainly in the right job!'

'*WHAT* did you say, girl?'

Miss Vipond twisted to glare at her. She wasn't a tall woman, but she was standing up and Milly was sitting in one of the hard plastic chairs. The teacher's hands on were on hips and she was scowling horribly. Milly steeled herself. 'I said you're in the right job, Miss.'

'*WHAT* do you mean by that? Are you insulting me?'

Charlie was looking as if he'd been stuffed. Across the classroom, William Proctor was giving her frantic looks accompanied by one-handed throat sawing motions. Milly gave him a reassuring smile.

'That depends on your point of view, Miss. In any other class I probably would be, because I'm saying you're rude. But as this is Defiance and Discourtesy, that's a big compliment.' She stopped for a moment to let Miss Vipond think about it. 'So really you should thank me. But if you did thank me, it would be polite, and that would mean that you weren't a good Discourtesy teacher. It's a big problem!'

Miss Vipond looked confused. 'Very well,' she said after a second. 'I'll give you the benefit of the doubt this time. Just come up here and help me hand out these Discourtesy textbooks, will you?'

Milly took a deep breath. 'No,' she said.

'NO? What in Hades do you mean, no?' Miss Vipond's face had taken on the colour of a ripe plum. It clashed unpleasantly with her drab dress and the fierce wall colour. Milly crossed her fingers beneath her desk.

'This is *Defiance* and Discourtesy. If I helped you when you asked me, that wouldn't be defiant – just the opposite. I think you're trying to catch me out.'

'Ha! Very good, Miss – Dillane, is it? A promising start, though I'd bet good money that you can't keep it up. Take ten house points.'

Milly smiled. 'Thanks, Miss. I'm not sure what house

I'm in yet, but when I find out I'll remind you about those house points.'

'What do you mean, you don't know which house you're in? You'd better find out, you cloth-eared nitwit. And if you ever thank me again, I'll put you in detention for the rest of your life! And as for you –' Miss Vipond glowered at Charlie. '– I'm watching you. You'd better be prepared to show some serious rudeness pretty quickly!'

-oOo-

At dinner that evening the main topic of conversation was how to steal something stupendous for the Lightfinger Trophy. Sophie the blackmailer reported that she'd persuaded some of the older kids to allow her to join their team and they were going window-shopping at the weekend.

William Proctor was being cagey about his plans. 'Let's just say that I too have joined forces with some older and more experienced felons. I'm confident that with their experience and my brain, we'll come up with something impressive!' Milly looked at Charlie with raised eyebrows but held her peace.

The only people with no ideas were Milly and Charlie. Walking back to their rooms, Charlie tackled the subject. 'I *hate* this stupid competition. I don't want to steal something. And neither do you. So how do we get out of it?'

Milly chewed thoughtfully on her thumbnail as she looked up at him. 'If we want to stay at Blaggard's, I think we'll have to go through with it. And I'm pretty sure we *do* want to stay, because the alternative is Crumley's, which makes Blaggard's look like a knitting club. So I've been thinking. What we need to do is steal something priceless that no one else wants. If no one wants it, no one will care if we pinch it.'

'Something priceless that no one wants? There's no such thing!' Charlie looked regretful.

Milly's eyes narrowed. 'I'm not so sure. Could we steal someone's reputation? Like Father Christmas, who's supposed to be fat and jolly. We could say that he wears a padded suit, and has anger issues.'

Seeing Charlie's look of doubt, Milly gave a nod. 'I agree. Too vague. And how could we present Lightfinger with a reputation? ... I've got it! We steal a Crown Jewel! The Queen's got masses of them. I bet she wouldn't miss one. My old Dependable History teacher was always saying the Crown Jewels belong to the nation, so it wouldn't even be stealing! Every tyrant from here to Hawaii would love their own Crown Jewel!'

'What about security? We can't just wander into the Tower of London, dump a crown in a bag and say that it was ours all along.'

'I'm sure I could think of a way round that, but it's just an idea. I'll come up with something. I'm not going to let Lightfinger ruin our lives for us,' Milly promised.

CHAPTER FOURTEEN

C harlie left Milly to her brainstorming. Her ideas were coming thick and fast – a discredited chemical formula for turning grains of sand into gold; a painting that everyone thought was a fake until it was suddenly discovered to be a lost masterpiece by Van Gogh. 'I could paint it myself, after lessons. He's my favourite artist!' she added. Charlie couldn't keep up and decided to ring his parents. Maybe they would have some advice about the competition, and if they didn't, he'd ask them how Gruffles was getting on. He'd make the call from his room, where there was no chance of being overheard.

Walking back, Charlie became aware of raised voices – an angry female one and a grovelling male one. The voices were loud enough to travel the length of one of the many corridors that branched off from the Reception area. Intrigued, Charlie followed them.

He passed a couple of classrooms. The door to the first one was decorated with a busy street scene. Skulking at one end was a sinister, black-clad figure, tailing a hapless

Dependable. *That must be the Stealth classroom,* Charlie deduced. Several metres further on, the next door showed a Blaggardian squinting through a magnifying glass at a pile of paper money on a workbench. Charlie stopped to consider it. *They look like twenty pound notes, and the little figure's wearing thick glasses – aha, got it! Forgery! The figure even looks a bit like Mr Molesworthy, the Forgery teacher!*

The puzzle solved, Charlie walked on. The voices were coming from the next classroom. He slowed as he approached it, taking care to walk as quietly as he could. The door was half open.

Charlie edged closer until he could see inside it. Although the raised voices were definitely coming from inside this room, he couldn't see their owners, who must be standing out of sight.

The first thing he noticed was a glossy poster, pinned to the wall near the door. The overhead lights were shining onto it, making it hard to read. Charlie moved forward a little so that he could make out the words: FAMOUS PLOTS THROUGH HISTORY – RATE THEIR SUCCESS! There were pictures of a couple of men in Roman togas with their arms around a smug looking man wearing a laurel wreath, and a bunch of men with pointy beards carrying little barrels marked 'DANGER – YE GUNNEPOWDER'. Charlie thought he could work those out – the assassins of Julius Caesar and the Gunpowder Plotters. But he scratched his head over a man dressed as a bear and carrying a long-handled axe, until the two figures in the room moved into sight and he forgot all about the poster.

The first figure he saw was Nick Lightfinger, grovelling

so abjectly that he seemed to have halved in height. 'Please, you must believe me,' he cringed. 'I have absolutely NO interest in your job. The idea's ridiculous...'

Ms Martinet stomped into sight. Her hands were on her hips and even from a distance, Charlie could make out the anger blazing in her eyes. 'Shut up. Sit down at this desk. Got a pen? *NO?* For Hades' sake! Go and get one!'

Lightfinger scuttled over to the teacher's desk, picked up a pen and then darted back to the desk indicated by Ms Martinet. 'At last. Now, write this out two hundred times. Best handwriting. If you make a mistake, *ab-so-lutely* any mistake at all, even the tiniest inkblot, you'll start again. Got it?' she barked.

Lightfinger nodded so fervently that Charlie thought that his head would fall off. 'Yes of course, Head Teacher. But really, I must continue to protest my innocence. Someone has set me up – a jealous teacher, probably.'

Ms Martinet dumped a sheaf of paper onto the desk in front of Lightfinger before turning to the whiteboard. 'Save your breath. I don't believe you. This is what I want you to write.'

In angry, slashing letters, she wrote on the whiteboard:

MS MARTINET IS <u>FAR</u> TOO YOUNG TO RETIRE. THE IDEA IS COMPLETELY PATHETIC, AS ANY IDIOT SHOULD KNOW.

'Bring it to my office when you've finished. And then I suggest you stay out of my way for a few weeks...'

Charlie crept away, wondering briefly if he should feel guilty.

Fat chance! he decided.

When he reached his room, he made his phone call. It was his mum who answered, which was unfortunate, because his dad was more sympathetic. But he was in the Hebrides looking for safe houses, apparently. Charlie outlined his concerns about the Thievery Competition and about Blaggard's in general.

Maisie Partridge's reaction was pretty much as he expected. 'You'll just have to try harder. I had a *wonderful* time at Blaggard's. And I won the "Future Famous Felon" award in my final year. As for the Thievery Competition – you're a Partridge, aren't you? Just pretend you're kidnapping something. You know where you'll end up if you're expelled, Charlie. Crumley's, like Great Uncle Edwin. He lasted three hours...'

And then Maisie Partridge dropped a bombshell: 'By the way, Gruffles has gone missing. He ran away. I *told* you to get him micro chipped. Don't worry, he'll turn up again. If not, there are plenty of other dogs. You can get a cleaner one, next time...'

Charlie rang off, his stomach twisting. *Thanks for nothing, Mum. And Gruffles has run away! How will he survive? He's not the sharpest tool in the box and he's never had to fend for himself. This is getting worse and worse!*

He reached for his laptop. It was his way of forgetting about life's problems and right now they seemed to be piling up with alarming speed. He surfed aimlessly for a bit and then hacked into the school's intranet system for some practise. He decided to send a love letter to Miss Vipond from Mr Borgia. *'You look like a beautiful pigeon in your grey dress. How I long to ruffle your feathers. And for once in my life, I'm not lying,'* he wrote, thinking what a good couple they'd make.

Then he started looking at hacking websites. One of his favourites mentioned a new site for aspiring hackers from age three and upwards. It was called *Perpetual Paradox*. It sounded interesting, Charlie thought, so he started to type the name into his browser. He'd got as far as *Perpetual Para-* when a long line of suggested links appeared. Automatically, he clicked on the first one.

-oOo-

Half an hour later Charlie was heading downstairs, laptop in hand. He needed to speak to Milly. She'd just sent him a text: *'In Library. Unusual place. Come & c.'* He stopped in Reception for a moment, trying to locate the Library. From one of the corridors he heard noises: animated voices, laughter and the crash and stutter of a dozen loud computer games. He set off in the direction of the sounds, halting outside a pair of scarred double doors. He pushed them open.

Presiding over the Library was a lavishly made up woman in a leopard print cardigan. Her badge identified her as *Miss Grimbly, Librarian*. The smile she unleashed on Charlie was ferocious. The doors slammed behind him, setting a marble statue of Sir Thomas Blaggard, surveying the room from an alcove above them, rocking dangerously.

Miss Grimbly smiled and batted her false eyelashes. 'Good try,' was all she said.

The Library was chaotic. Staggered in a circle around the room were cases stuffed to the ceiling with battered books. Tables were strewn around at irregular angles. Down one side of the room was a bank of computers, occupied by Blaggardians who were playing games at full volume.

Jet Mannington was leaning against a wall, trying to impress a group of girls. 'Pecunia Badpenny rang to speak to my dad the other day. She does it a lot. They're old school friends,' he was saying, with obvious pride. Everyone seemed to be intent on obeying the huge notices warning that:

SILENCE

WILL NOT

BE

TOLERATED

Charlie set off towards Milly. She was sitting slightly apart from a group of Year Sevens who were watching Agatha Quint demonstrate escapology techniques with two pairs of handcuffs and an upturned table. She gave him a big smile. 'Charlie, what's up? Come and watch Agatha. She's pretty good. Pity she doesn't want to be friends!'

Charlie looked at her with narrowed eyes. She seemed almost too happy. Like she was covering something up. 'Anything wrong, Milly?' he asked.

"Course not! What could possibly be wrong?'

'Come over here, then. This is important. Have you heard of Pros and Cons? I expect your mum uses them for – whatever it is that she does. It's *the* site for recruiting criminals to do your dirty work for you. Take a look at this.'

He repeated the actions he'd taken in his bedroom. 'I ended up on this dating website – Perpetual Paradise. It was an accident, obviously,' he added quickly. 'It looked weird and for ages I couldn't work out why. And then I realised. See this soppy looking woman? She's meant to be a librarian.'

Milly leaned over him, frowning as she read the librarian's introduction: *Hello, my name is Belinda. I'm seeking a very special gentleman who can share my interests. I'm a professional librarian, very passionate about books and about conserving them. My hobbies are Sudoku and amateur electronics...*

'She sounds as mad as a sack of marmosets, but I don't see what's bugging you,' Milly said.

Charlie pointed at the photo. It showed a woman smiling coyly as she 'conserved' a ragged book. 'I wouldn't want her looking after *my* books,' he said.

A drill was being inserted into the book's spine. A dentist's drill, by the look of it. 'I see what you mean. That's just wrong. Who mends books with a drill?' Milly asked.

Charlie gave a mysterious smile and double-clicked on the point of the drill. Immediately the page dissolved in a swathe of screen flames and a stark message appeared: Welcome to Pros and Cons, **_the_** site for matching world-class professional tyrants with reliable convicts, criminals and stooges. Your computer's credentials are now being checked. If it's not registered to a recognised felon, a self-destruct sequence will commence that will reduce your computer to mush. If your computer is police-registered, not only will it be reduced to mush, it will also explode directly afterwards. You've been warned...

CHAPTER FIFTEEN

C harlie caught Milly's look of alarm. 'Don't worry. This laptop's registered to my dad. He's well known in all the worst circles.' He clicked on the SHADY SITUATIONS VACANT/SOUGHT tab at the top of the page. A long list of job specs appeared. Milly skimmed through them: – *henchmen required for family intimidation business; operatives needed to assist in illegal venture – big rewards anticipated; first-rate plotter seeking challenging non-Dependable employment.*

Charlie pointed to an ad near the bottom of the list: *'Highly intelligent robotics expert required to aid top-notch criminal in realising daring, world-changing scheme. Flexible morals a definite requirement. Only the best will be considered. If you think this could be YOU, work out how to progress to the next page. DON'T waste my time!'*

Charlie gave Milly a lop-sided grin. 'I thought the ad was a bit long-winded, so I played around with it. Watch this!' His fingers flew. In no time he'd clicked on the first letters of the words 'expert', 'notch', 'criminal', 'realising',

'YOU', 'progress' and 'time', spelling the word ENCRYPT. The page seemed to dissolve. Charlie quickly turned down his laptop's volume.

A new page appeared. It featured a film clip of a woman, speaking straight to camera. She was thin-faced, flat haired and her lips were a slash of vermillion. Her eyes were lashless and bored. The only interesting feature on her face was a thick monobrow, darker than her pale hair. Milly thought that it seemed to crawl across her forehead like a furry caterpillar and her fingers itched for a pencil and some paper to draw her that way, with a segmented insect body and dozens of spindly legs. 'Pecunia Badpenny!' Milly exclaimed.

Charlie nodded. 'Weird how someone can look boring and scary at the same time,' he said.

Badpenny was thrown into insignificance by the creature behind her. It bore a passing resemblance to a large dog, but it was made from gleaming black metal. And with its bullet-shaped head, caterpillar tracks instead of legs and multiple barbed tails probing the air like Medusa's snakes, it was a dog out of a nightmare. It hovered effortlessly above Badpenny – her own personal thundercloud.

'Hellfire, what's that?' Milly gasped.

'Interesting, isn't it?' Charlie was fascinated. 'Some form of robot. Maybe even an A.I.'

'A what?'

'An A.I. – Artificial Intelligence. Capable of making its own decisions.'

Milly grimaced. 'Scary thought!'

'I suppose so. I'd love to have a go at re-programming

it. I bet Mum would love it – a dog with no hair, who never gets dirty.'

The villain on the screen began speaking. Her girlish voice didn't match her appearance. 'You know who I am. If you don't know that I'm the most feared villain in the country, you're not the person I'm looking for. Go away now,' she said.

There was a short pause. Badpenny looked down. She seemed to be smoothing her hands, which were off screen. Then she looked up again and continued. 'My congratulations on making it this far. You're obviously an excellent problem solver. That's one of the qualities I'm looking for. There are others. I need someone with up-to-the-minute knowledge of computing and technology. Someone who isn't afraid to experiment. Someone, like myself, who doesn't concern themselves with minor irritations like the law.'

She paused again and then leaned in, so close to the camera that Charlie could count the pores on her nose. 'There's one other thing. Don't bother applying if you're frightened of being responsible for some ... shocking changes. Especially in relation to a certain criminal school in Borage Bagpuize that's in need of some drastic modernisation.

'Oh, and don't even think about warning the school. If you do, my Wolf here will use his unique skills to track you down and make you extremely sorry. That's a promise.' Badpenny touched the creature's shining head. She was wearing peculiar gloves that looked as if they were made from black and white animal skin. The Wolf flinched away from her touch. Its soulless eyes flashed red.

After a long stare into the camera, Badpenny leaned forward and switched it off. The screen went dark for a few moments, and then a white text box appeared. It was headed: 'Apply here ONLY if you are EXTREMELY serious about this position.' The cursor flashing inside the text box was skull-shaped.

'What on earth is she planning? How can she be sure that someone from Blaggard's won't see her advert? Why is she wearing those awful gloves?' Milly's voice was rising. Heads were turning, trying to tune in to what she was saying.

Charlie shot her a look of warning. 'Shhh! We should keep this to ourselves for now. Blaggard's is famous for being rubbish at turning out decent hackers, so I suppose she feels safe. And the gloves – they're made of panda skin. She has them smuggled out of China because –' he shrugged – 'because she can. She says they're the ultimate sign of her success. I've managed to hack into the replies to her ad.'

Only four courageous people had put themselves forward as potential employees. Each candidate had sent a photo of themselves, a CV and a letter outlining their previous crimes.

'This is the bloke who got the job. Herman Blight,' Charlie said. He called up the details of a man with scruffy blonde hair. His eyes weren't quite looking into the camera.

'He's pretty well known in techno-crime circles. He's even got a fan page on Crimbook – they call him the Wild-Haired

Wizard. He's a genius. There's a great story about a floor lamp that he made into a remote-controlled assassin. I'd *love* to get my hands on it and take it to the *Robbery Roadshow*. Gavin McGlintock would be gobsmacked!'

'How old is this ad? It was near the bottom of the list of jobs, so it can't be that recent,' Milly said.

'Three or four months, at least.'

'We need to find out what she's planning. Or rather you do – you're the hacking genius. And no pressure, but you need to do it fast, before Badpenny can make her "shocking changes" to Blaggard's.'

CHAPTER SIXTEEN

Milly spent the next few days keeping Charlie focused as he battled Badpenny's stupendous online security, and her eyes and ears open for signs that the threatened plot had been launched. In Milly's mind, every thin, pale haired female over five feet tall started to take on a resemblance to Pecunia Badpenny. And some of the males, too.

On top of this, there were lessons to contend with. They weren't exactly impressing their teachers. Earlier that day, they both failed spectacularly in their very first Betrayal test. They'd hardly scored any marks at all, causing the teacher, the dapper Marius Babington, to jump up and down on his beautiful jacket and suggest that they'd be better off joining the Borage Bagpuize Brownies.

Milly was also wrestling with a personal problem that she hadn't shared. She'd become aware of it when she'd gone to the Library and signed into her emails, the same night that Charlie had found out about Badpenny's evil intentions towards Blaggard's. There was a new message from her parents. *Maybe Dad's started a new forgery. Or Mum's got a new amazing present from some criminal she's saved from a horrible fate!* She was eager to read their news.

Dear Milly,

How are you? I hope you're settling in at Blaggard's, but I suspect you're not. I've received an email, you see. An anonymous email. It said that you've got secret Dependable leanings and an aversion to stealing. The sender thought we ought to know. Have you made an enemy?

I have to confess that I'd had suspicions, and I did worry that your love of art might tempt you towards the straight and narrow, but it seemed too incredible to be true. But if that's the way it is, I hope, I trust, that you'd be able to confide in me. I can't deny it would be a blow, but we'd get over it.

Now I need to ask you a question – I've started looking at alternative schools. Dependable ones. Would you prefer to go to one of these? They're bound to have mile-long waiting lists, but you know me, there isn't a waiting list in existence that I can't jump.

I haven't mentioned this to your father
yet. You know how proud he is of his
Blaggard's connections. But if you
say yes, I'll tell him and we'll move
forward. All of us. We are your parents
and we love you, no matter what.

Love Mum. Xxxxx

Milly felt the blood draining from her face. She looked up to see Jet. There was a satisfied smile on his face. *Of course! Revenge for the bucket thing. He's probably tried the same trick with Charlie's family, but knowing Charlie's high-tech security, his message wouldn't get through... I'll have to think of some way of getting my own back... I'm not going to a Dependable school! For a start, Mum and Dad would be devastated. And anyway, it's MY future and I'll sort it out for myself. I'm not being dictated to by Jet Mannington, or anyone else!*

She stared blindly at the bookshelf labelled *Advanced Discourtesy – SIXTH FORMERS ONLY* as she imagined her parents facing the future with a Dependable daughter. An image of her mother popped into her mind. Tears smeared Dymphna's immaculate make up and her self-assurance had dissolved. Then she thought of her father. Lovable, loopy Arthur simply wouldn't understand.

She imagined them sipping lukewarm tea and being ignored by the Dependable parents at Dependable School Open Day. They would be outcasts.

Out of the corner of her eye she could see that Jet was

still smiling expectantly. *I'm not giving up. The other schools will still be there if I change my mind. If I want to move, it'll be when I'm ready. I'm not going anywhere. Not yet, anyway.*

Quickly, she sent off a reply.

```
Dear Mum, please don't worry - it's
a mean trick being played by someone
I upset the other day. You should be
proud of me - my first real enemy! And
I've only been here a few days! I think
it might be a new school record in
enemy making.

I'm settling in pretty well. I've
already made a good friend. His name's
Charlie and he's a techno-whizz. He's
one of the kidnapping Partridges,
although they've got into cyber crime
now. I think you were at school with
his mum and dad? There's a new Thievery
competition that we're going to enter
together. We're really excited about
it. So I'll say thanks but no thanks
to the Dependable schools, and stay at
Blaggard's. Infamy here I come!

Luv Milly ☺ Xxxx
```

She made sure that she gave Jet a dazzling smile that she hoped would really bug him. Before she could log off, a reply from her mum pinged into her inbox.

OK, I'll take your word for it. But I
know you better than anyone, Milly.
Your stubbornness might just turn out
to be your downfall. Think about that.
If you'd be happier elsewhere, don't
leave it till it's too late. xxxxx

Worries about the impending Thievery competition were also nagging at Milly. Most students had teamed up by now, and rumours were flying about who was going to steal what. Milly and Charlie discussed it in the lunch queue.

'I heard Jet Mannington – you know – Bucket Boy – boasting about his plan,' Milly said. 'He reckons his dad's a famous robber. Jet's based his plan on the one his dad used to steal the famous Purple Pearl of Pimlico from that singer who'd had it inserted into one of his false teeth. The teeth were in a glass in a bank vault at the time.

'Jet's got his sister, Shady, working on it. And William Proctor too. They've pinched William's dad's armoured car. They're going to ram-raid the National Felony Museum and steal the only copy of Sir Thomas Blaggard's autobiography. I reckon it's pretty well priceless to the criminal world. Duck, Charlie!' Milly bobbed down to avoid a low-flying bread roll that someone had smuggled away from the serving counters.

Charlie didn't duck. Automatically, he stuck out a long arm, caught the bread roll and sent it zooming into a breadbasket at the other end of the serving area. It landed with a neat plunk. There was a burst of applause and hoots of appreciation from the other diners.

'It's a reflex,' Charlie explained, with a blush at Milly's look of admiration. 'I was top scorer in the basketball team at my old school.'

Milly shook her head in wonder. 'That's amazing!' Then she continued: 'William Proctor reckons it was Lightfinger who told them to pinch the book cos it's the most valuable thing he could think of. It wouldn't be Jet's idea – his idea of a good book would be *Noddy Goes Berserk at Bathtime!*'

Charlie flushed with anger. 'That's cheating. No help from adults, it says in the rules.'

'Don't be dim! This is Blaggard's! Cheating's expected. We're more likely to get into trouble if we *don't* cheat. William says Jet and Lightfinger are weird allies of some sort. And we know who Lightfinger's least favourite students are, don't we? He'll hold a really dull party if we're expelled for coming last.'

-oOo-

That night Charlie was in his room, making notes on abuse from his Discourtesy textbook. Miss Vipond had proved true to her word – she *was* watching him and constantly trying to catch him being polite. He'd asked Milly for advice.

'Take her off her guard. As soon as she sets foot in the classroom, start flinging insults at her. That'll shut her up,' Milly had suggested.

Charlie bit the tip of his tongue as he considered each insult. *'Nice dress. Did you buy it in a camping shop?'* Yep, I like that one. *'Oh, were you talking to me? I was thinking about something more interesting.'* Might be a bit subtle for Miss Vipond. *'You smell like a burglar's underpants.'* Nice! I'm definitely using that one!' He smiled and drew a star against it.

A sudden loud THUD banged against his window, sending him leaping off his bed.

Out of nowhere there came another THUD, followed by the sound of frantic scrambling. Charlie jumped up and peered into the blackness. At first all he could see was the town of Borage Bagpuize – a mass of lights twinkling against the blue-black sky. Beyond it, Crumley's School for Career Criminals crouched on its hill, more gargoyle than building.

Then a ghostly shape cannoned towards him. It splatted against his window and dropped out of sight. As Charlie's eyes adjusted, he made out Gruffles shivering on the fire escape.

Charlie felt a surge of joy at the sight of his pet. 'Gruffles! How did you get here? What are you doing, you stupid dog?'

He opened his window. Gruffles scrambled through the window, knocking his master off his feet and leaping around him in a joyful dance. He looked like a filthy but athletic sheep. Ignoring his pet's odour, Charlie hugged him tight, feeling the sharp spars of his ribs. 'You're as thin as a jailbird on hunger strike! When was the last time you ate?'

A sudden knock on the door made both boy and dog jump.

'QUIET!' Charlie hissed, and bundled the struggling animal into his wardrobe.

CHAPTER SEVENTEEN

'What have you got in there? It smells awful!' Milly said, taking a step backwards.

She raised one eyebrow as Charlie pulled her into his room, slammed the door and opened his wardrobe with a weary flourish. Gruffles bounced out. She groaned. 'Great. That's just what we need. Well, that explains the smell. He looks hungry. Starving, actually. I'll get him some food. We need to work out what we're going to do with him.'

'I don't think I can send him home. He'll only run away again. He hates living with my mum.'

I don't think Gruffles is the only one. Better not say anything, Milly thought. She hurried to the kitchen, returning a few minutes later with a plate of cold chicken nuggets. 'The door wasn't locked. There's a note on it saying that they've gone to a disco for lonely cooks – hope that's more fun than it sounds. At least the food should be good.'

As Gruffles attacked his meal, Milly and Charlie sat down to discuss tactics.

'I've just had an idea,' Milly said. 'Gruffles can stay in your room, or in mine if there's an inspection of the boys' rooms. William Proctor says they never inspect the boys' and girls' rooms together, after the first day of term. During the day he can run around the woods –' She intercepted a look of confusion on Charlie's face. 'No, Charlie, I mean Gruffles, not William! Hardly anyone goes there, except Ms Martinet.

'I'm going to start a rumour about a ghostly dog. It's a good job that Gruffles is white. Whitish. I'll report it to Mr Borgia in confidence. That's if I can winkle him away from Miss Vipond. Have you noticed how lovey-dovey they've been in the last day or two? I nearly walked straight into the pair of them in the Stealth section at the Library yesterday – holding hands and giving each other gooey glances. Yuk!'

She saw a look of satisfaction cross Charlie's face. 'Why are you looking so pleased? What have you been up to? Actually, don't tell me. I don't want to know! Anyway, I'll tell Borgia that I think it's the ghost of Sir Bryon de Bohun's hound, Humbug. In a day or two, the whole school will know about the ghost dog and be too scared to do anything about it. Good job Humbug's reputation is so fierce.'

Charlie drummed his fingers on the lid of his laptop as he considered the plan. 'But why's the dog haunting the woods in daytime? Ghosts usually come out at night.

Milly frowned. 'I didn't think of that... Hang on, I know – because Ms Martinet likes walking there. Even ghosts don't want to meet Ms Martinet in the dead of night.'

'But what about his smell? Do ghosts smell?'

'I don't see why not. If anyone notices we'll say it's the

stench of the tomb. You'll have to start wearing extra-pongy deodorant, to mask his smell in your room. What do you think?'

'Fantastic! You should be top of the class in Plotting.'

Milly's eyes crinkled. 'Don't hold your breath! Let's keep Gruffles in for the night – he looks tired. We'll let him out early tomorrow. That'll be my first sighting of the ghost dog.'

A few days later, things were turning out just as Milly had predicted. People were slowly getting used to *Prowling Panther*, Charlie's new deodorant that promised to '*bring the danger of the jungle to your armpits*', and the ghost dog had become a Blaggard's legend. Everyone *knew* that it had been haunting the grounds for the best part of two hundred years. William Proctor was heard explaining that the first sighting of the phantom pooch had been on 14th January 1822 at a few minutes past midnight, but now Ms Martinet had taken to strolling in the woods, it preferred to do its haunting during the hours of daylight.

Gruffles was more or less free to wander at will. *We've just got to hope that no one starts wondering why a massive black dog like Humbug would come back as a much smaller white one. And that no one catches him cocking his leg against a tree. Or worse. Don't think I could explain that away,* Milly thought with a grimace.

-oOo-

Halfway through the next day's Plotting lesson, Milly felt her mobile phone vibrate against her leg. She edged the phone out of her trousers and quickly ensured that Ms

Martinet wasn't looking. She was in luck. The teacher was facing the whiteboard as she outlined their homework.

'I repeat, so there's *ab-so-lutely* no excuse for poor work: your homework is on page 19 of "Practical Plotting to CCSE Level".' Without turning round, she said, 'William Proctor, explain CCSE, please.'

Proctor looked pleased. 'It's the Criminal Certificate in Secondary Education, Miss. Taken at the age of sixteen and founded in 19-'

'Yes, thank you. Shut up. Everyone, go to page 17 and look at Question One: 'Prepare your first draft of a detailed plan to stage a take-over at your school. Present your plans as bullet points. Ensure they are chronological.' Does everyone know what chronological means?' The Head Teacher whipped around.

Milly froze in the process of calling up her message. Fortunately, there were several rows of trainee criminals in front of her and the phone was on her knees, below desk-level. Ms Martinet couldn't see it, but Milly's stillness caught the Head's attention.

'Milly Dillane. You look like a burglar caught in a spotlight. I don't know what you're doing, but you'd better stop. Tell us the meaning of chronological.'

'It means in order of time, Miss. So if the first thing you'd do is go to the Head's Office to overpower her, make that your first bullet point.'

'Correct. You're sharper than you look, which isn't hard. Now I want you all to take this task seriously. The best plan will be forming the basis of a practical run-through later in the term...'

As Ms Martinet turned back to the whiteboard to finish outlining their homework, Milly rolled her eyes in relief, then flicked a look at her phone. The message was from Charlie, who was in one of his extra Hacking classes. *'I think I'm in! Not str8 4ward tho. Tell u 2night.* Milly stuffed the phone back into her trouser pocket, lifting her head just in time.

'... and be warned,' Ms Martinet was saying. 'If you don't want to be put on weekend detention for the rest of your school lives, make sure that your suggestions relating to the fate of the Head Teacher are respectful. Any questions?'

No one dared ask one.

CHAPTER EIGHTEEN

Milly poked her head round Charlie's door. He was flopping on his bed, still tiptoeing through Badpenny's online files. 'Any luck getting through those firewall thingies?' she asked.

'Some. It's the hardest thing I've ever done. I'm not gonna let it beat me, though. I've never been defeated yet. My pride as a hacker's at stake!' He gave a weary smile. 'There's just one more thing I need to work out. A map. I think it's important but it keeps chucking me out. And Gruffles is still in the woods! Give me a minute to get him...' He hauled himself to his feet and stretched his long body. Milly pushed him back.

'Forget that. I'll get Gruffles. You carry on.' Then she was gone.

Charlie rubbed his red eyes and returned to the battle. He was beginning to take risks. He'd try anything to get through this never-ending task. Suddenly his screen went red. Ghostly music began snaking from it. Badpenny's face flashed onto the screen. A flashing skull was superimposed over it.

'You. I'm tracking you down. I'm going to slit you open and wrap your entrails round a broom handle.' Badpenny grinned. Flames shot from her eyes and mouth. The music changed to a funeral march and Charlie's laptop fizzled and died.

'Argh! A booby-trap! I'm an idiot!' He tossed the computer to one side and thumped the bed.

Milly stomped back in, dragging Gruffles. 'Your dog's a menace. I've been chasing him round the woods in the rain. He was after a little tabby cat. I'm sure some of those trees are fake – one of them was buzzing and I think there was a camera hole in the trunk.'

She stopped glaring at Gruffles and looked at Charlie. 'What's happened?'

'The map file was booby-trapped. It's fried my computer and Badpenny knows she's been hacked. She's going to trace me and then – she wants to kill me. Horribly.'

Milly's eyes widened. 'How long will it take her to track you down?'

'There's some good news, I suppose. I protected my identity pretty thoroughly. It's going to take a couple days before she works out that her hacker isn't a Tibetan yak breeder,' he gave Milly the ghost of a grin. 'And then it'll be another day or two while she traces me back to England.'

He reached over to this little desk and picked up a slim pile of paper. 'Anyway, I've got something to show you. In Hacking today, I got into Badpenny's private online diary. You'll enjoy this – she calls it *"Musings of a Criminal*

Mastermind". I reckon she's dreaming about publishing it,' Charlie rolled his eyes. 'While Mrs Prye – the Advanced Hacking Teacher – was distracted, I sent some of the most useful bits to print in an empty classroom. Listen to this.'

Charlie placed one finger across the gap between his eyebrows, improvising a monobrow. He put on a high voice that was a passable copy of Badpenny's, and read aloud: *'Since I was a small girl, daydreaming about world domination, one person has stood in my way. We were at Blaggard's together, where she made it her goal to thwart me. When I was due to receive an award for outstanding Discourtesy, she was so rude to the Discourtesy teacher that he ran away the day before I was due to collect it. When I came up with a sure-fire way of rigging the Future Famous Felon competition in our final year, I'm convinced that she persuaded the judges to "miscount" the votes so that a second-rate kidnapper with a cleaning obsession won instead.*

'Even after we finished our tyrannical training, Griselda Martinet remained a thorn in my side, criticising my most brilliant plans. She only became Head Teacher of Blaggard's because she knew I wanted that job myself.'

'OK. So, Badpenny hates Ms Martinet and it looks as if Ms Martinet hates her back. What else?'

'I'll skip a few pages ... plans to become Prime Minister ... designs for stamps with her face on them – yikes – ah, here goes: *"At last the time has come to get my revenge on Griselda Martinet and the school that favoured her over me. With a teensy amount of help from Herman Blight, I have designed a device that will ... I won't reveal that just yet. It's*

*in my secret hideout, awaiting testing. Blaggard's will be
my testing ground and my first Blaggardian guinea pig will
be Griselda Martinet. When I've fine-tuned my device and
destroyed my enemy, I'll take my rightful place as Head of
the school.*

*"Blaggard's will become the truly evil establishment that
it should be. I'll remove the wishy-washy subjects and replace
them with proper ones. Blaggardians will be waving goodbye
to Fabrication and Defiance and Discourtesy, and hello to
Poison Pen Letters – Which Poison? And Assassination
Techniques Using the Contents of a Lunch Box.*

*"At long last, Blaggard's will be turning out proper
criminals. And that's just the beginning. Once they're properly
trained, they'll be put to very good use! I'm not expecting
them to live long, but there's plenty more where they came
from." '*

There was a shocked silence. 'With Badpenny in charge,
Blaggard's will make Crumley's look like a Dependable
crèche! So, what are we going to do about it?' Milly said.

Charlie hunched one shoulder. 'We're two kids and a dog
whose main interest in life is chasing his own tail. There's
nothing we can do.'

'I don't believe that. We can have a go, anyway. It's better
than just standing by while Badpenny turns Blaggard's into
a school for psychopaths. Think about that last bit you read
to me. Where will she go for her next batch of slaves? She
hated our parents when they were at school. I bet they're
pretty high on her list of victims.'

'...I hadn't thought of that. Well, whatever the evil thingy
is, it's ready for testing. She's sent Herman Blight an email

asking him to meet her at her secret hideout. If I was him, I wouldn't trust her an inch!'

'Me neither. If she's really planning to publish those mad memoirs, she won't want Blight saying that he was the real inventor of the thingy. Have they met up yet? Where's this secret hideout of hers?' Milly asked.

'They're going to meet soon. That's all I know. And the location of her hideout – that was the map I was trying to look at when she fried my computer. There was one thing I made out for sure though...' Charlie hesitated.

'What? '

'Badpenny's lair – it's somewhere in Blaggard's.'

Milly gave a grudging smile. 'That's clever! Cancel your plans for the next few days. We're going to search this school from top to bottom. We've got a mad villain's secret lair to uncover.'

CHAPTER NINETEEN

Two days later, Milly and Charlie had managed to examine nearly every room in Blaggard's, at break times and after lessons. There was just one room left, and only a burbling lunatic would enter it willingly. *I'd better start burbling,* Milly thought. Straightening her shoulders, she knocked on Ms Martinet's door. The Head Teacher opened it so fast that Milly jumped.

'Miss Dillane. Come in... What do you want?'

Milly had been looking aghast at the black walls and endless framed photos covering nearly every inch of them. She dragged her gaze back to Ms Martinet. 'It's about Plotting homework – the plan to take over the school. I think the most important thing will be to make sure that you're out of action. You're the cold heart and brains of Blaggard's. If you're secured, everyone else will follow. So I need to check that you don't have a secret way out of your office. The last thing I'd need is for you to jump out of a hidden door, just as I'm about to take over!'

The Head Teacher gave her a twisted smile. 'I didn't

know that you had such grand ambitions. I'm heartened to hear it. Come back after lunch, but you won't have long. My time is precious.'

Milly thanked her and turned to leave, but as she touched the door Ms Martinet's purring voice stopped her. 'One moment, Miss Dillane. Come and sit down for a second.'

Reluctantly, Milly lowered herself into one of the chairs arranged in front of Ms Martinet's huge desk. The seat was knobbly and uncomfortable – like sitting in the lap of a skeleton. Ms Martinet sank into her own generously padded chair with a sigh of pleasure. Then she put away the numerous documents littering the desk, leaned forward and subjected Milly to a long stare. Milly decided she'd better stare back. Eventually Ms Martinet spoke.

'How are you settling into Blaggard's? A number of your teachers have mentioned you. Tell me, which lessons do you most enjoy? Have you formed any plans about what form of law-breaking you'd like to enter when you're older?'

Thoughts chased each other through Milly's head. *There's no chance those teachers have been telling her how great I am. They'll have been moaning about my lack of criminal enthusiasm. Probably pushing her to get rid of me. But I'm not giving up. So what should I say?... I like Ms Martinet. And weirdly enough, I trust her. I know she's pretty hard, but I don't think she's malicious. I'll try telling her the truth. Or some of it, at least.*

Out of the Head Teacher's sight, she crossed her fingers. 'I don't know, Miss,' she said.

Ms Martinet frowned. 'What? What don't you know?'

'Anything. I don't know what I think of Blaggard's. I don't know which lessons I enjoy. And I don't know what I want to be when I grow up. I don't even know if I want to be a criminal! I'm hoping that Blaggard's will help me decide.'

Ms Martinet drew back. 'You are either remarkably clever or remarkably stupid. Why are you telling me this? Why aren't you lying to me?'

'You can't fool a fooler, Miss. You're an expert. You've already got doubts about me – that's why we're having this talk. If I told you a bunch of lies, you'd spot them in a second. Then you'd expel me.' Milly gave a tiny smile. 'I'm pretty competitive. I don't like losing. Or failing. And I'm not going to fail at Blaggard's, if I can help it. Maybe you can do what it says in the school prospectus – dig around and drag the criminality out of me. With parents like mine, it must be in there, somewhere.'

'Hmmm... "Remarkably clever" might just be the most accurate assessment of you.' Ms Martinet gave her a long stare. '...Very well. I've never been one to back down from a challenge. I accept. I'm going to be watching you closely for signs of criminal potential. When I've made up my mind, you'll be the first to know. You should go now, before I have second thoughts.'

Charlie whistled when Milly told him about the conversation. 'I don't know whether to high five you or lock you up for your own safety!' he said.

'Let's hope it was worth it. We're running out of places to search,' Milly replied.

CHAPTER TWENTY

They arrived at the Head Teacher's office at the appointed time to find Ms Martinet prowling the corridor.

'I hope you don't mind if Charlie helps me search. Someone told him that you keep the bones of a student who failed his Plotting exam manacled against your wall.' Milly Fabricated. 'I told him it wasn't true, but he was still a bit worried about it. So I brought him along to check it out for himself. I didn't want him developing a phobia or anything.'

Charlie took his cue. He peered fearfully over Ms Martinet's shoulder, as if the skeleton of the mythical student was about to drag open her office door and throw itself onto him.

'You're quite safe, Mr Partridge. I keep all the bones and bodies in one of the outhouses,' Ms Martinet said, straight faced. 'You've got fifteen minutes while I go and see an informant. There are rumours about an imminent Crumleian raid on Blaggard's. Possibly with inside help. We don't want any Crumleians shambling round the school, causing death and destruction!'

When she was gone and they were alone in Ms Martinet's office, Charlie looked around. 'Yikes! It's like the Chamber of Horrors,' he said. 'A pile of student bones would fit in very nicely.'

'Yep. Even grimmer than I'd realised,' Milly said. The photos she'd noticed earlier turned out to be framed wanted posters and mug shots of Blaggardians who'd hit the heights of villainy. *Most of them aren't very attractive,* Milly reflected. *And that's being kind to them.*

The slab of a desk was bare now, except for a locked diary that looked as if it guarded all sorts of hair-raising secrets, and a mug tree from which a few spare masks and sets of skeleton keys were hanging. Suspended from the wall was a set of rusty leg irons with a dangling iron ball the size of a melon. Near the back wall loomed a set of black screens, like giant bat wings. The only welcoming object was Ms Martinet's big chair. It was draped in soft, fleecy throws that seemed to beckon Milly to curl up in them.

Charlie started checking the walls while Milly ducked behind the screens to see what they might be concealing. It wasn't long before Charlie stopped at a large, plain cupboard that was pushed against the back wall. It was as tall as the room, and it was legless. There was a sign on the door: 'DANGER – Confiscated Items.' He opened the door and peered inside. It wasn't long before he called out, 'this cupboard. It's... weird.'

Milly ducked under Charlie's arm to take a look. 'The contents are pretty weird, if that's what you mean. I wonder who brought that sword to school? Or this creepy-looking bottle?' She picked it up and held it up to the light. 'Look – it's poison! Do you think Miss Vipond brought it in, to poison polite students?'

'No. I mean yes, she probably did, but that's not what I mean. Look at the back. The tip of that sword disappears behind the back panels.' He backed out of the cupboard to check out the wall it was leaning against. 'It's fastened really carefully to the wall. You can't even look behind it. So, where does the tip of that sword go? I reckon this cupboard is hiding a secret room.'

The back of the cupboard sounded hollow when knocked, but Milly and Charlie couldn't work out how to reveal the space they were sure must be behind it. There were no hidden levers or buttons disguised as bits of carving. It was a perfectly plain cupboard. They spent a frustrating few minutes pushing and then trying to forcibly shove every component of the wood, but nothing worked.

'We're running out of time. We'll have to think of an excuse for coming back and have another go at it,' Milly said, eventually.

'Argh, this is annoying! We haven't got a cat in hell's chance of getting it open before....' Charlie's voice petered out. The back of the cupboard was slowly sliding upwards, revealing a dark area behind it. The sword that had betrayed the existence of the hidden space toppled into it. The back panel disappeared from sight. Then, much faster than it had vanished, it slid into place again.

'It must be voice activated – programmed to open when

someone says certain words. Say what you said again, Charlie. Slowly,' Milly instructed.

'I said – This is annoying ... I think you're right... we haven't got... a cat in hell... AHA! The password must be CAT IN HELL!' The panel slid up again, revealing a black space. Charlie took a step forwards and squinted.

Immediately the panel started closing again. 'CAT IN HELL!' Milly called, before he could disappear into the darkness. 'What can you see?'

Charlie shook his head. 'Nothing. It's empty. Just a stupid, shallow, empty wooden cupboard.'

Milly peered under Charlie's arm. 'Why hide an empty closet?' She ducked inside and peered closely at it. It didn't take long for her to realise that one of the sidewalls of this new cupboard was hollow.

'Another hidden room. This is like a rabbit warren! So there's another door to get through. No levers or buttons, as far as I can see, which means there must be another password to find. How does Ms Martinet's mind work?'

Charlie thought. 'Well, she's scary, we know that. And she loves Blaggard's. How about BLAGGARD'S FOREVER?' Nothing happened. 'BLAGGARD'S RULES?... BLAGGARD'S IS BEST? Bah!'

'We need to hurry up. We've got about five minutes left. So – what else do we know about her? She hates Crumley's. She says it's a school for scumbags – aha!'

The wall on the left-hand side slid up and away, just like the previous one. Charlie slipped into the new space.

'Well?' Milly demanded, craning to look round him.

Charlie gave a little choke. 'Nothing useful. But I think Ms Martinet's got a guilty secret. Look!'

The new cupboard was stacked high with colourful magazines. Charlie picked one up. *Kitten Lovers' Weekly*. Ms Martinet – a secret kitten lover! And look!'

The back wall of the dark den was plastered with posters of adorable, blue-eyed kittens. Grey kittens, brown kittens, white kittens, black kittens, ginger kittens and tortoiseshell kittens. Placed centrally on the back wall was a faded photograph of a yellow-eyed tabby cat, in a highly polished silver frame.

'No wonder she hides these. Her reputation as a terrifying dictator would be ruined if it came out that she's soppy about kittens.' He ran a finger over the framed photo. 'This must be her childhood pet... Careful Milly! There's a bowl of food on the floor. She's definitely got some cats stashed away somewhere. I wonder where they are?'

'Good question,' Milly said, sidestepping the bowl of cat nuggets. 'Maybe she's hidden them in a drawer in her desk? Let's close the cupboard before she returns. We won't tell anyone. In a weird way, it makes me respect her more. She's human, after all.'

By the time Ms Martinet returned, looking slightly anxious, the secret doors were closed and Milly and Charlie were finishing their examination of a different part of the room.

'Thanks, Miss. We're confident that if we locked you in here, you'd stay put. And Charlie's not *quite* so worried about failing his Plotting exam now,' Milly said with an innocent smile.

CHAPTER TWENTY-ONE

O ne look at Ms Martinet's glowering face, as she took up her usual position for Assembly two days later, told Milly that she had bad news to announce. She could guess what it was.

'Good morning, future felons,' the Head Teacher said, without the glimmer of a smile. 'I have the result of the ballot to find the name of the new house. All the suggestions have been considered and counted by reliable judges. Well, by Mr Molesworthy and Miss Vipond. And Mr Borgia offered to help but we didn't trust him.' Behind her, Edgar Borgia assumed a look of wronged innocence.

'There were several hundred entries. We had to weed out all the votes from a certain student who kept voting for himself – really, Harry Blackmore, you need to apply some intelligence to your exploits. Next time you want to fix a ballot, do alter your handwriting on some of them.' A tall, blond Year 10 grinned proudly at his friends. One of them patted him on the back.

'I'll announce the result in reverse order,' Ms Martinet

continued. 'In third place, with 208 votes, is Mitch McTavish. An excellent choice, and I only wish that more of you had been intelligent enough to vote for him.

'In second place, with 281 votes, is, ahem, Martinet. I can only thank you for the honour. William Proctor, I suspect that many of these entries came from you and they demonstrate your unusual intelligence.'

Proctor beamed.

'And so to our winner. With 376 votes, and with Miss Vipond and Mr Molesworthy eager to expose me if I Fabricated, I couldn't pretend that someone else had won. The winner is, unfortunately... Pecunia Badpenny.' There was a ripple of applause.

'I've been in contact with Badpenny,' Ms Martinet continued. 'She'll be coming to Blaggard's tomorrow to pick the first captain of Badpenny House. I know you'll extend her a hearty welcome. Heartier than she deserves, in my opinion.'

Milly nodded to herself. It was what she'd been expecting. It was the perfect excuse for Badpenny to prowl around the school, unhampered.

Ms Martinet leapt off the stage and left the Assembly Hall without a backwards glance.

-oOo-

It was early the following morning, and Charlie was hurriedly removing evidence of Gruffles from his room.

The previous evening, Milly had overheard Mrs Christie and Ms Martinet discussing an imminent inspection of the boys' rooms. She'd warned Charlie immediately, and had arrived early to bundle a struggling Gruffles down the fire escape and into the woods. But Charlie was tired after the long, frustrating search for Badpenny's hideout, and he was finding it hard to concentrate.

'Right – the window's opened and I've sprayed the deodorant, although it smells worse than Gruffles. I've got rid of the dog hairs. And the dog!' He was ticking things off on his fingers. 'I *think* that's everything.' He was only just in time. There was a sharp knock on his door.

Mrs Christie had only been in his room for a few seconds, with a handkerchief against her nose to filter the odour of *Prowling Panther*, before she frowned and pointed at a large sack, leaning against the wall. The name *'LEAP!'* was printed on its front in big letters, accompanied by pictures of bouncing hounds. It was unmistakably, undeniably dog food.

Charlie could have kicked himself. He'd bought it the previous day, so that Gruffles could have a good breakfast before starting his day's haunting, and he'd forgotten to hide it.

'Is there something you're not telling us, Charlie dear? I do hope that you haven't acquired a pet? I'd be forced – reluctantly of course – to drop you into a whole world of trouble.' Mrs Christie's eyebrows were drawn into a perplexed line.

For a second Charlie's mind went blank; then it leapt into action: 'Actually, Miss, they're for me. I've got a dog at home – he loves this food. Eats it all the time. One day in the holidays I was hungry, and I'd been reading what it says on the bag. Here, look: 'Builds strong bones and teeth, makes your pet leap with vitality!' And I thought, 'I'd like strong bones and teeth,' and I was feeling a bit tired, so I tried one. It was delicious! So I've bought myself a bag. When I get the midnight munchies, I just help myself. My teeth feel a lot stronger now. Look!'

He bared his teeth.

There was a long silence.

'In fact I think I'll have one now. Fancy one?' He picked up the bag, gave it a good shake and offered it to her. She took one gingerly and waited for Charlie to pick one too. He made a show of turning over the brown nuggets before settling on a knobbly one. He closed his eyes and put it in his mouth. 'Mmmm. Delicious. What do you think?'

Slowly, Mrs Christie inserted the dog biscuit into her mouth. Reluctantly, she began to chew. Her eyes bulged. She put one hand over her tightly closed lips.

'Want another one?' asked Charlie, helping himself.

'Ugh, no! What a peculiar young man you are. I'll just suggest that you buy a less powerful deodorant as a matter of urgency, and I'll be on my way.' With a flash of her flowery overall, she was gone.

Charlie let out a long whistle. *Maybe I'm beginning to get the hang of this criminal thing. Or at least the Fabrication side of it!* And it could have been worse, he supposed. At least she hadn't spotted the dusty bone sticking out from under his bed. *I wouldn't fancy chewing on that.*

CHAPTER TWENTY-TWO

The following morning, Milly and Charlie entered the Assembly Hall to the buzz of excited chatter, as Blaggardians anticipated their first glimpse of the notorious Pecunia Badpenny.

They didn't have long to wait. Ms Martinet had just taken up her position on the stage and opened her mouth when the doors were thrown open. Badpenny marched in. She was dressed in a black jumpsuit that Milly thought made her look like a knobbly stick that had fallen into a fire. There was a ripple of nervous applause but Badpenny ignored it, fixing her eyes on the grim-faced Head Teacher.

A collective gasp flew round the hall as the watchers saw the creature accompanying her. Flying a few paces behind her, just higher than head level, was the metallic wolf that Milly and Charlie had seen in the Pros and Cons film clip. In real life it was even more menacing. Its pointed head moved restlessly as it assessed the crowd and its barbed tails darted like angry serpents. They seemed to taste the air. The fact that it flew silently only added to its menace.

Nearly all the Blaggardians strained away in their seats as Badpenny and her creature approached the stage. Charlie was the exception. Milly watched him lean closer, his eyes roaming admiringly over the robot. *He looks like my dad when he sees a masterpiece. Almost hungry!* Milly thought.

Badpenny's gaze never left Ms Martinet as she mounted the steps. The Wolf flew from one side of the room and then back, scanning the crowd, before coming to a stop just behind his mistress. There was a moment of awkward silence and then Ms Martinet extended a stiff hand. 'Pecunia. Welcome.'

Badpenny didn't move, making Milly wonder if she going to ignore Ms Martinet completely. Then she sighed. 'Griselda. You're looking worn out.' Her voice dripped ice.

Milly watched a little pantomime of politeness unfold. Badpenny took Ms Martinet's outstretched hand as if it was made of something unspeakable, shook it briefly and then dropped it. She wiped her gloved hands on her trousers. 'I'm expecting great things of my visit to Blaggard's. It should prove to be extremely educational,' she said.

'Perhaps you'd like to address a few words to the students who've afforded you this honour,' suggested Ms Martinet, through clenched teeth.

'Of course. I was planning on doing so.' Badpenny turned and stepped directly in front of Ms Martinet.

'Tyrants of tomorrow, thank you for having the perception and intelligence to pick me. I'm looking forward to repaying your kindness.'

Milly raised her eyebrows at Charlie. He grimaced.

Badpenny peered around at the Assembly Hall with an

expression of boredom. 'I'll be staying for a couple of days, to find the first captain of Badpenny House,' she continued. 'I'm an excellent judge of character and I'll be watching every one of you.'

Without looking behind her, she snapped her fingers. The Wolf zipped to a halt in front of her. 'You'll soon grow accustomed to the presence of the Wolf. He's my devoted bodyguard. As long as you treat me with respect, he's harmless. Of course, if you plan to upset me in any way, it's a different story, ha, ha.'

No one laughed. Badpenny sighed again and stomped down the steps. She started for the exit, her eyes roving over the nervous crowd. Milly seemed to catch Badpenny's eye and for a second the criminal glared at her. The Wolf stopped too, its tails quivering in Milly's direction. When Badpenny had passed by, Milly and Charlie exchanged a look of alarm. 'What was that all about?' Charlie mouthed.

Milly shrugged and shook her head.

Edgar Borgia had arrived a little late and had been standing near the doors to check his form's register on the handprint detectors. When he saw that Badpenny was bearing down on him, he blenched and tried to step out of her way. Badpenny sidestepped too, in the same direction. They did an awkward little dance that ended when the villain grabbed him by his tank top and hauled him out of her way. 'Wolf! Follow me!' she called over her shoulder, as she shoved open the doors.

If a flying robot creature could flinch, the Wolf did. Its attention had been fixed on one of the windows that looked out onto the woods. Its ears and tails had lifted. Badpenny snarled at it. 'Are you deaf as well as useless? I mean NOW! Unless you want to be sold off to a gang of arms dealers to use as target practise?'

For a second the Wolf's eyes flashed red. Then it zipped through the closing doors and after Badpenny, leaving students and teachers to stare at each other in nervous silence.

CHAPTER TWENTY-THREE

After dinner, Milly and Charlie went to the Library to kill time until lights out. The room was dark and relatively quiet for a change – it was movie night and most of the Blaggardians were mesmerised by the film being projected onto the wall-size screen. William Proctor had explained that it was one of Miss Grimbly's favourites – *Revenge Sumo-Style* – the tale of a group of huge men in uncomfortable-looking nappies who liked to do away with their enemies by jumping on them from great heights, squidging them flat.

To one side, Agatha Quint was quietly explaining the best way of escape for potential victims of an enraged sumo. 'Baby oil. Loads of it. All over. Or cooking oil. When he squeezes you or jumps on you, you'll splurge away faster than an overripe banana that's been run over by a bus...'

Next to Agatha, William Proctor was determinedly trying to take notes in the dark. He underlined the word 'overripe' and highlighted it in yellow. Then he added a quick sketch of what looked like a man made from pillows with his arms around a matchstick with legs. Peering over William's shoulder, Milly decided that art wasn't his strong point.

After a while, Milly and Charlie moved their chairs to the back of the room to talk quietly. Milly glanced around quickly to make sure no one was listening, then leaned towards Charlie.

'If I was a villain with an evil invention to test and only two days to do it in, I'd want to get on with it as soon as possible,' she said quietly, keeping her eyes on the screen. 'That means tonight. Badpenny's staying in one of the guest cottages. We're going to follow her and stop her.'

In the film, a mountainous sumo was climbing up a ladder. Beneath him, a shackled man looked wildly around, perhaps hoping to spot a bottle of baby oil. Charlie winced as the sumo launched himself from the top of the ladder. 'What about the Wolf? It could reduce us to mincemeat in the time it takes a safe cracker to pick a bike lock,' he said.

'I think we've got a secret weapon when it comes to the Wolf – Gruffles. I've been watching the Wolf. Badpenny's horrible to it and I think it's fed up. Gruffles could show it that being a dog doesn't have to mean terrorising people. He could appeal to its better nature. Befriend it, maybe.'

Charlie seemed to have developed a nasty cough. 'Better nature? *The Wolf*? Have you been dipping into the secret flask of sherry that Mrs Christie keeps in her overall pocket?' He thought for a moment. 'Of course, if I had a chance to reprogram him, I could sort him out. I've been building a Compassion Chip, to install some kindness into him. I just need to get my hands on him.'

'Maybe you could install one in Badpenny too? I wish there was time for that. Sadly there isn't, so we'll just have to rely on *GRUFFLES* doing what he's told, when he's told.' Milly gave a humourless laugh. 'And there's something else. Something that you're not going to like. We're going to let her capture us.'

-oOo-

It was later still, and Blaggard's had settled down for the night. Milly and Charlie had been waiting in the woods with Gruffles for what seemed like hours. A sliver of light told them that the cottage door was opening. A knobbly silhouette appeared and merged into the darkness as the door closed again. They heard the figure moving away. 'Come on,' Milly mouthed. She started after Badpenny.

With Gruffles being helpful for once, it wasn't hard to keep tabs on the villain's progress. They tracked her through the woods and round the back of the school. They proceeded warily. 'It's important that she doesn't catch us too soon. We need to get inside her den, first,' Milly whispered.

There was no sign of the Wolf, but every second Milly expected to hear a whoosh as the robot dog descended on them with light blasting from its cold eyes. Its absence worried her. *Why isn't it here? We're counting on it... Maybe it's lying in wait somewhere? I hope so. Of all the weird things to hope for!* Her heart was in her mouth as she crept onwards.

Badpenny came to a halt at the back entrance to the kitchen. They saw the flash of her white face as she switched on a torch to sort through a set of keys. She unlocked the door and disappeared through it.

Before Badpenny turned off her torch, the air above her rippled, like a breeze on still water. Charlie put his hand on Milly's shoulder. 'Did you see...?' he murmured.

But Milly was already moving. 'I don't know what it was. Maybe it was nothing! We'll have to worry about it later. She mustn't get away!'

Once they were inside, tailing Badpenny got harder. The straight corridors meant that cover was limited and Milly and Charlie had to drop back and wait for their target to round a corner before they could move.

It was also much scarier in the dark and they flinched at a display of stocking masks used in famous robberies. By day, they had looked a little forlorn, even slightly ridiculous. But by the light of the moon, as a cloud shifted away from it, they took on the appearance of a row of melted faces.

After some nerve-tearing minutes, they heard the sound of a door being pushed open.

'She's gone into the Assembly Hall,' Charlie muttered.

They waited. When nothing had happened for two or three dragging minutes, Milly moved forward.

'Come on. We're going in,' she said.

CHAPTER TWENTY-FOUR

T he Assembly Hall was even more unsettling than the corridors. By day it was just a big room, but in the darkness the empty space seemed endless. Even though Milly knew that there was very little cover in the room, it felt as if someone was hiding just out of sight, waiting for the perfect moment to jump out on them. The sound of Charlie's shallow breathing told her that he was feeling something similar.

As the friends struggled to make sense of their surroundings, they caught sight of a pale face with strange, unevenly set eyes, grinning at them through the gloom. Charlie gave a little gasp. 'It's OK. It's just Sir Bryon de Bohun in his glass case,' Milly muttered.

They edged around the walls, eyes probing the darkness. Progress was achingly slow, and there was a nasty moment when Gruffles walked into the display cabinet containing Sir Thomas Blaggard's long johns. To Milly and Charlie, the resulting thud and whimper were as loud as a burglar dropping a crowbar from a great height. They stopped, holding their breath. Milly was listening so keenly, it seemed to hurt her ears.

Nothing.

They set off again. Eventually, their outstretched hands touched the glass case that housed Sir Bryon.

'What's going on?' Charlie whispered. 'This case has moved.'

As their eyes adjusted a little, they saw that Sir Bryon and his glass coffin were now at a strange angle. And instead of the wall that was usually behind him, there was a black, rectangular gap. Footsteps were coming from it, gradually becoming fainter. They seemed to be moving downwards. There was a whining creak, as if something heavy was being pushed. A few seconds later, the sequence of sounds was repeated.

A little gingerly, Milly edged forward to inspect it.

'*Of course*! A tunnel. Great place to hide it! No-one's gonna go poking around behind Sir Bryon. The floor slopes downwards. When I said this place was a rabbit warren, I wasn't kidding. I'm surprised the whole building hasn't collapsed... Ready? We've got to get after Badpenny. We don't know where this leads to, and we mustn't lose her.'

Before Charlie had the chance to reply, she'd crept into the gaping blackness.

-oOo-

The temperature dropped immediately. The air smelt stale and old. Milly stretched out her hands and found that she could touch the walls on either side of her without difficulty. Her questing fingers felt the rough regularity of bricks, draped with chilly cobwebs that seemed to clutch at her.

Milly realised that the floor felt different. She reached down to feel it. It was strewn with crisp wood shavings that crunched beneath their feet. *Good. Now we want Badpenny to hear us.*

The pair groped their way onward and gently downward, but they had to stop again almost immediately. A grainy slab was blocking their way. A door. Milly pushed it and it creaked open.

Beyond was more blackness, even denser if that was possible. They moved on. Charlie stumbled over Gruffles in the darkness. The dog yelped.

'Good idea, pretending to trip. She's got to hear that,' Milly said.

Charlie gave a low, embarrassed laugh.

Again and again a door blocked their way. They would push through it, only to encounter yet another one. It was maddening. After what seemed like hours, their fumbling fingers met with a door that felt different. It was punctured with metal studs that seemed to be forming some kind of pattern. Milly listened, but the only sound she could detect was Gruffles, panting gently. She pushed the door open and peered inside.

It opened into a long room. The walls were covered with wood panelling. Candle stubs in two brass sconces threw feeble, flickering light that travelled only a short distance into the darkness before giving up. Draped from the candle sconces, cobwebs made tatty curtains that stirred now and then in some undetectable breeze.

After a moment's hesitation the friends stepped inside. The room was nearly empty, except for a table standing against one wall. It should have been dusty, but the top looked as if it had been cleaned. Candlelight was glowing dimly on its surface. Lying on it was something surprising. A pair of headphones. They looked super-cool – deepest black, with a logo and flashes of luminous lightning on the padded ear cups.

Charlie was drawn to them like a burglar to an open window. He drifted past Milly, picked them up and examined the logo. 'Hay-Zee,' he read out loud. 'Never heard of them, which is weird, because I thought I knew all the cool brands. And these are supercool, though there's nowhere to attach your connector cable.'

He turned them over before slipping them onto his ears. 'They're really comfortable. I bet the sound quality's amazing. I'd love to try them out properly...'

A new voice sounded from the far end of the long room.

'Then your wish is about to be granted!'

A searing light cut through the gloom, revealing Badpenny, standing in front of an open door. The smirk on her face was hideously highlighted by the glow of her torch. Charlie couldn't prevent his stomach from turning a somersault, even though this was all part of Milly's plan.

The villain approached him unhurriedly. The strange ripples in the air shadowed her movements. She reached up and twitched the headphones from his head. 'You! I thought it must be, but – a Blaggardian hacking expert! I thought those advanced hacking lessons were just a way of giving Mrs Prye some free time!

'Still, I'm pleased that it's you – Charlie Partridge – son of my hated rival, Maisie Liversedge. At last I can pay her back for snatching the Future Famous Felon award from me,' Badpenny smirked.

'I've got a file on every Blaggardian, past and present, and I looked you up,' she continued. 'You're just a one-trick pony – clever at hacking but utterly lacking in the instincts of a true criminal. Nothing more than a performing monkey, really.' Badpenny curled her lip at him.

Charlie searched his mind for a cutting retort, but all he could think of were the insults he'd noted down to use on Miss Vipond. *They'll have to do. Here goes.* 'Nice dress. Did you get it in a camping shop?' he blurted out.

Badpenny looked down at her trousered legs and then back up at his face. 'Are you blind as well as stupid?' she enquired. 'Does it look like I'm wearing a dress?'

'Well... whatever you're wearing, you smell like a burglar's underpants.' Charlie wasn't going to give up without a fight.

That seemed to do the trick. Badpenny flushed and glared. 'Do you remember what I promised to do to you when I found out you'd been hacking into my private affairs? When I've finished with you, Charlie Partridge, you'll be *begging* me to wrap your entrails round a broom handle!' She shoved him towards Milly.

'And here's Milly Dillane – completely out of her depth and desperately trying to live up to the standards of her parents. How's your father, by the way? He never *quite* got over our encounter in that locked classroom all those years ago. Such a sensitive boy!'

Milly lifted her chin to look into the villain's eyes. 'He's never mentioned that to me. He must've forgotten it,' she Fabricated. 'I'll tell him you were asking after him, though. He has that effect on everyone. No one ever forgets Dad. Not even *decades* after he's forgotten them completely!'

Badpenny's smile dissolved. 'You're lying. And you're not very good at it. Very shortly, you'll be wishing you'd never heard of me, let alone tried to defy me.'

'In your dreams!' Charlie put his hands on his hips. 'We've got a secret weapon. Gruffles is an attack dog – trained to go for the jugular of anyone I don't like.' He looked down. 'Oh, hellfire!'

The 'attack dog' had chosen that moment to roll onto his back for a tummy scratch. He looked up at Charlie and waved his legs in the air, in a way that he clearly thought was irresistible.

Badpenny smirked. 'The only frightening thing about your dog is his smell! Did you really think I'd come on a job like this without my protector? Wolf! It's time to show yourself. And get a move on!'

The waves in the air intensified. They started to solidify and darken. In a few seconds the Wolf was hovering there, glinting by candlelight, eyes glowing with menace.

'Do you remember my mentioning that the Wolf had hidden talents?' Badpenny asked, rubbing her hands together. 'Invisibility is just one of them. One of the more pleasant ones, as you'll find out shortly.'

CHAPTER TWENTY-FIVE

With the Wolf circling them like a hungry hyena, Badpenny prodded Milly and Charlie through the long room and into another one. And then another. The chain of rooms and tunnels seemed to be never-ending.

'Sir Bryon de Bohun had this built,' Badpenny said. 'The design is a work of genius – there are secret doors all over the school. I'm the only one who knows where they are.' There was a possessive gleam in her eyes as she stretched out a skinny arm to illustrate the extent of her domain.

'The tunnels are so thin, they're undetectable from the outside, but the bricks are extra thick, for sound-proofing,' she continued. 'They lead down to a very private set of rooms, beneath the school. Believe me, no one will hear you when the screaming starts...' She stopped for a moment to let this sink in. Milly and Charlie exchanged glances of fake dismay.

'Sir Bryon blackmailed his Head Master to turn a blind eye to the construction work. He used the rooms to entertain an exclusive club, open to only the wickedest Blaggardians. He called it the Brotherhood of Brimstone. I'm sure he'd *love* my current use of his den.' The smile on Badpenny's face was complacent.

Then she looked at Milly. 'Are you a reader? Your sidekick doesn't strike me as a bookworm.' She curled her lip at Charlie. 'Don't you hate that bit in spy stories where the villain tells his entire plan to his captured enemy, as he prepares to kill them?' Badpenny shook her head in disapproval. 'And then the wretched enemy escapes, armed with the knowledge of exactly how to stop the villain.'

But you're going to do that anyway, because you're mad and hopelessly vain and you can't resist boasting. Which is what we're counting on, Charlie thought.

'I've always despised that part of the plot,' Badpenny didn't wait for an answer. 'And I'm not going to act so stupidly. But I *would* like you to witness my genius at work. It's so seldom that the work of a criminal mastermind receives the recognition it deserves.'

Milly gave her a fake sympathetic smile. 'Poor you! Why don't you start up a charity instead – Support for Unpopular Criminals. You'd be really appreciated, then. You could just call it SUC, for short.' Charlie couldn't suppress a smile of admiration.

Badpenny's eyes sparked. 'You think you're funny, but you won't be joking in a few minutes. First though, I've prepared a demonstration for you.'

They'd reached another door. Like the previous one it was decorated with metal studs. Now there was enough light to make out the pattern. It was the word *BoB* in big, curling script. 'The Brotherhood of Brimstone,' Milly breathed, as Badpenny turned a big key and herded them into an adjoining cell.

And there they found Ms Martinet, gagged and trussed up like a chicken ready for the pot and dumped in a heavy wooden chair. *Hellfire! This isn't part of the plan,* Charlie thought. Milly made a move towards the Head Teacher, but after a jab from Badpenny's elbow, the Wolf zoomed over Milly's head and hovered menacingly between them.

'I went to Griselda's office after lessons, pretending that I wanted to consult her about the captain for Badpenny house,' the villain said. 'She seemed to be distracted by something – kept muttering about being too busy to talk because she'd lost her noodles! Perhaps noodles is her pathetic slang for brainpower, which would be uncannily perceptive of her, ha, ha...'

No one laughed. Charlie thought that the Wolf looked embarrassed, if that was possible. Griselda Martinet glared at her enemy.

Badpenny didn't seem to notice. 'I had the Wolf with me and it performed a little immobilising trick. It uses rays of light – quite ingenious! Then it transported her here through a secret door in that disgusting kitten cupboard of hers. I bet she's never even stopped to wonder *why* there are secret cupboards in her office, let alone explored them.' She wrinkled her nose disdainfully at Ms Martinet.

'I hope you realise how lucky you are,' Badpenny continued. 'You're about to witness the first trial of my magnificent invention! You didn't realise it, Charlie Partridge, but you've been wearing something unique and unimaginably powerful. Yes, you were wearing ... my Hay-Zee headphones!'

She flourished the headphones with pride.

A long silence followed.

Charlie pulled an unimpressed face and raised his eyebrows.

Milly laughed. 'You're even madder than you look! What're you going to do – play her a tune she doesn't like? That'll *really* teach her a lesson.'

'No, you dreary Dependable. I'm going to wipe her mind! From now on, she'll be my slave!'

Badpenny fitted the headphones lovingly over Ms Martinet's head. Then she stood back and smiled at her. 'Are you ready, Griselda? Say goodbye to your mind. Don't worry. I'll go easy on you. I won't turn the volume up full. That would reduce you to a puddle of mush on the floor. Just a gentle flick of the switch....'

To Charlie, it seemed as if the headphones came to life. They clamped themselves over Ms Martinet's ears. Their lightning flashes strobed and gave out a high-pitched hum that seemed to worm its way inside his brain. He could only imagine what it would feel like when the noise was magnified by the earphones.

Griselda Martinet seemed to be resisting with every fibre of her being. Her hands gripped the arms of the chair and the sinews in her neck stood out as she fought for her mind. But eventually she stiffened. Her eyes bulged. She gave a final glare at her enemy, then her body slumped like a puppet whose strings have been cut.

'Perfect!' Badpenny's laugh was disturbingly girlish.

'I've got big plans for my headphones. Once I'm Head of Blaggard's, I'm going to create my own private criminal army. They'll do anything I want – robbery, kidnapping, murder. Lots of murder. And the first "volunteers" to join it will be Blaggard's students, brainwashed to remove any lingering shred of decency.'

'That's pathetic. How can a few hundred kids, even brainwashed ones, stand up to a proper army?' Milly asked, curling her lip.

'Your lack of imagination is depressing. I've acquired a factory that will soon be turning out thousands of pairs of headphones. I'll be distributing them – free of charge – to the British army and police force – gifts from an anonymous admirer. In a month or two, the whole country will be at my command!'

Badpenny pushed Milly towards the still figure of the Head Teacher. 'You're welcome to try to revive my new slave. I assure you, she's beyond human help. I'll even untie her!' She pulled at the knots securing Ms Martinet's bonds. The ropes thudded to the floor. The Head Teacher seemed not to notice that she was now free. 'Griselda, stand up.'

Ms Martinet shambled to her feet. Milly took one of her cold hands and thought for a moment. 'Miss, I know you can hear me. I need to tell you about something that happened today. A group of Blaggardians raided the Jewel House at the Tower of London and got captured. The Tower ravens are really guard-birds – their beaks are specially sharpened. The Blaggardians are in hospital now, being treated for nasty pecks. They've told the police about Blaggard's true identity.'

The Head Teacher didn't even blink. Milly bit her lip. Badpenny gave a satisfied simper. 'You see? Mindless. Well, I think it's time to put an end to your laughable attempts to thwart me. You're shortly going to experience another of the Wolf's talents. Rather an unpleasant one.'

CHAPTER TWENTY-SIX

Badpenny led the way out of the cell. With the Wolf jostling them, Milly and Charlie had no choice but to follow.

Milly decided that it was time to bring Gruffles into the action. *I'll have to work out how to bring Ms Martinet back, later.* 'I'm sure you won't mind answering a question for us,' she said to Badpenny. It's what always happens in the spy stories, just before the good guys get ... you know.'

'Hurry up, then. I've got a busy night ahead of me,' Badpenny said, pushing back her piebald glove to look at her watch.

'Well, what bugs me is the Wolf. Why aren't you nicer to him? I've had umbrellas I've been kinder to than you are to him. I think all he wants to do is play, maybe with Gruffles. *He* loves having fun. Don't you worry that the worm – sorry, Wolf – will turn on you?'

Milly gave the Wolf a sympathetic smile. It slid closer to Badpenny, its tails quivering. Badpenny batted it away, sneering at Milly. 'How pathetically weak you are. It isn't a "he". It's an it. A concoction of wire and circuits. Why would I bother being pleasant to a machine?'

The Wolf's eyes turned darkest blue. Badpenny rubbed her hands together. 'Enough of your witless questions. I'll begin by brainwashing your gangling sidekick. I don't think I'm going to bother brainwashing you, Milly Dillane. That way, you'll know exactly what's happening when the Wolf turns his special talents on you.'

'Wolf, when I've finished with the boy, dissolve them both. Slowly and painfully. Start at their feet and work upwards – it'll take longer.' Badpenny threw the order behind her. 'Before you die, spare a thought for your families. They'll be receiving some of my headphones *very* soon.

'Oh, and Wolf – don't forget to finish off that evil-smelling excuse for a dog.' She looked around the dingy room. 'Where *is* the dog?'

Gruffles was nowhere to be seen.

'So much for relying on Gruffles. Is there a Plan B?' Charlie asked.

Milly couldn't think of an answer.

The Wolf was turning slowly towards them. The light in its eyes began to change to red. The colour intensified. Badpenny approached Charlie slowly, holding the headphones in both hands. She settled them on Charlie's head as reverently as an archbishop crowning a new king. Milly made a move towards her friend, but a flash of the Wolf's scarlet eyes stopped her.

'Miaow?' A small tabby cat stepped delicately into the room, tail waving.

Gruffles had returned to Ms Martinet's cell and was nibbling a dusty bone, but when he realised there was a cat nearby, he sprang to life. He pounced back into the long room, lips curling away from his teeth. The cat hissed and crouched. For a moment the two ancient enemies stared at each other, waiting to see who would break first. Gruffles gave way. He hurled himself at the cat, barking furiously. The cat screeched and took to its paws. With Gruffles snapping at its tail, it hared out of the room.

For a second, the Wolf hovered uncertainly. It looked from Badpenny, to Milly and Charlie. Then, with a *PERP* of joy, it hurtled after the racing animals.

'WOOLF! Come back here. I've had enough of you. When this job is finished, I'm melting you down,' Badpenny screeched. She snatched the headphones back from Charlie's head as she spoke.

The Wolf halted. It paused for a second and then returned to Badpenny's side. It turned to face Milly and Charlie, crimson light glowing in its eyes. Then it stopped. Slowly, ever so slowly, it spun round to the gloating Badpenny. The look of triumph congealed on her face.

The light in the Wolf's eyes started pulsing. It was accompanied by a droning noise that built up until it throbbed. The noise stopped suddenly. In the quickest of flashes, a ball of piercing white light flew from its eyes. It stretched and lengthened and then fell over Badpenny. She froze in mid stride, engulfed in a bright cone of light. And there she stayed.

'Is she dead?' Charlie spluttered.

Milly approached the frozen villain. In the bright light

her face looked ghastly, her mouth wide open, either to scream or spit out a further order. Milly blew into Badpenny's eyes. She blinked. 'No, she's not dead. Just frozen. The Wolf's come back to bite her. Ha!'

They looked at the Wolf. It had shut off the beam of light, although the white cone imprisoning Badpenny held true. They approached the gleaming creature. It floated warily, assessing them. Milly extended a gentle hand and stroked the Wolf's head.

'Thanks, Wolf. We'd like to be your friends. Do you want to come with us? You don't have to stay with Badpenny. There's lots of other things you can do that are much more fun.'

The Wolf's eyes glowed yellow for a second. It gave Milly a gentle head-butt. 'Great. That's settled then. We've got some things to sort out, but we need some information first. How long have we got until Badpenny can move again?'

The Wolf's eyes threw out a single blast of white light.

'An hour? That's not long.'

The Wolf perped in agreement.

'Good job I brought these along, then!' from out of her back pocket, Milly brought a pair of handcuffs. They were enamelled in black and white stripes. She gave a slightly guilty grin. 'I pinched them from Agatha Quint. I was going to give them back, in a day or two. She annoyed me – there's no need for her to be so unfriendly! Anyway, they'll be put to good use now.'

She turned to the Wolf. 'Wolf, do you think you could put these onto Badpenny? For a bit of extra security?'

It seemed that the Wolf was only too happy to add to Badpenny's humiliation. A pair of telescopic pincers appeared from the region of its chest. They grabbed the handcuffs, extended them through the prison of light and fastened them round Badpenny's thin wrists.

'Perfect!' Milly said, as the Wolf did a happy little bounce in the air.

Charlie pulled a little plastic box out of his trouser pocket and opened it.

'Wolf? I've made something for you. A microchip. It'll make you a lot happier. And it won't hurt you or alter your powers at all. Would you let me install it? It'll only take a sec,' as he spoke he was removing an intricate flake of metal from the box.

The Wolf hesitated.

'I promise you'll be fine,' Charlie said. 'Dependable's honour.'

The Wolf studied his face for a few moments. Then it perped. A second later, a little metal door in its chest popped open and a matchbox sized compartment slid out.

'Thanks,' Charlie said. From another trouser pocket, he produced another box containing a set of miniature tools – screwdrivers and tweezers other things whose use was beyond Milly.

'I dread to think what else you've stashed in your pockets,' she commented.

'Not much. Just some useful bits and pieces,' Charlie was frowning with concentration as he began his task.

Installing the chip was the work of a few minutes. Finally, the compartment slid back into the Wolf's chest and a shudder ran the length of its body. Its ears stood on end. It looped the loop. The light in its eyes changed from red to yellow to pink to green to purple, in quick succession.

'There. I've installed my compassion chip.' There was a ring of satisfaction in Charlie's voice. 'What now?'

Milly was already moving forward. 'There are more rooms to check out. And then we need to find Gruffles and that cat. I think we're gonna need it.'

The other rooms turned out to be more cells, all with their keys still in the locks. One contained a cowering Edgar Borgia, the Fabrication teacher. He'd tried to melt into a corner when his cell door opened, but he soon recovered himself.

'Ah – I was imprisoned by the Wolf just as I was about to capture Badpenny. I've been planning an ingenious escape since then. I was just about to put it into action, actually, but since you've gone to the trouble of coming to get me, it would be rude of me to refuse...' he quavered.

Milly lifted a disbelieving eyebrow.

Borgia gave a sickly smile. 'OK, she forced me down here with that fiendish Wolf. She said she'd acquired a strong-minded guinea pig to try out her brainwashing thingy, and she wanted to see what it would do to someone at the other end of the intelligence spectrum – someone "not far off brain-dead" were her words. Can't imagine why she chose me.'

The occupant of the other cell was less surprising. Lying on a bench and staring at the cobwebby ceiling was Herman Blight, Badpenny's hired techno-genius. 'Am I glad to see you! Badpenny double-crossed me. She was going to brainwash me!' His voice was full of indignation. 'I was second on her brainwashing list – straight after Griselda Martinet. I wasn't even her first choice of victim! Unbelievable!'

Blight was grateful for being rescued and claimed that while he'd been doing some thinking. 'I don't think *actual* crime pays. Although don't tell anyone I said that, guys, will you? I thought I might apply to Griselda Martinet for a teaching job.'

Mention of the Head Teacher reminded Milly that she needed their help. But first she had to coax Borgia from his cell. When he'd emerged and seen the Wolf, he'd scrambled back. It was only when Milly told the trembling teacher that he could hide behind Charlie that he crept out again.

'Do you know, I think the Wolf deserves a nicer name? What do you reckon?' Milly asked. Charlie and Blight nodded. Ms Martinet just stood with her nose against the wall. The Wolf gave a hopeful *perp?*

'How about Rover? Fido? Bonzo?' called Borgia, from behind Charlie.

The Wolf's ears drooped.

Charlie had a flash of inspiration. 'Nice suggestions, Sir, but I don't think he likes them,' he said tactfully. 'How about Wolfie? That's a cool name. Sort of friendly and dangerous at the same time.'

The Wolf gave another, perkier, *perp.*

'That's settled then. Wolfie it is,' Milly declared.

CHAPTER TWENTY-SEVEN

With Milly's permission, Wolfie carried out a final act of revenge against Badpenny. He wrapped another beam of light around her and turned her upside down. Then he swung her backwards and forwards, like a human pendulum. Her face turned green. After a stomach-churning minute or two, he dumped her on the floor and *perped* rudely in her face before heading for the door.

It was a strange little queue that filed past the glaring villain. In front flew Wolfie, lighting the way. Then came Milly with Herman Blight, who was trying to tell her more about his own brilliance. Milly was ignoring him, looking out for potential threats.

Following Blight was Griselda Martinet, as docile as a tame lamb. Bringing up the rear, and occasionally prodding Ms Martinet when she became overly fascinated with the walls, was Charlie with Edgar Borgia. The Fabrication teacher was deep in a story about how he'd saved a group of people from a much eviller rogue. 'I don't want to boast, but this particular villain made Badpenny look like Mary Poppins...' his voice whined on and on.

Milly imagined Charlie's frustration as he listened to Borgia's endless Fabrications. *Bet he's wishing that Badpenny had brainwashed Borgia when she had the chance. I'd tell him to keep quiet, but Charlie's too polite for his own good. Come on, Charlie!* She willed her friend to say something. And then she heard Charlie give a little cough. 'Sir, do me a favour and keep it for later, will you? I need to listen out for danger,' he said.

'Of course. Remind me and I'll tell you the rest when we're safe,' Borgia replied. Milly smiled to herself and threw a quick glance behind her. There was now a definite spring in Charlie's step.

They found Gruffles in one of the outer rooms, pacing under a dusty shelf on which the tabby cat was crouching, fur sticking out like a cartoon explosion. Charlie grabbed his dog's collar and hauled him away, leaving Milly to soothe the cat before picking it up. She carried it to Ms Martinet, who was staring at the floor.

Milly extended the cat towards the Head Teacher. It purred happily. Ms Martinet's head twitched. Milly held her breath, but no spark of recognition leapt into the teacher's unblinking eyes.

'Mr Blight – isn't there anything you can do?' Charlie asked. 'You invented the headphones in the first place!'

Blight shrugged and smiled his unreliable smile. 'Sorry, guys. I didn't get that far. Badpenny wasn't interested in reversing the process.'

Ms Martinet's arms had been hanging limply by her

sides. Now Milly pulled them until they were extending outwards. Then she pushed them backwards so that they bent at the elbows. Finally, she turned them palms up and pulled them together. It was like arranging a showroom dummy.

Very gently, Milly placed the cat into Ms Martinet's upturned hands. She pushed them until it was nestled against the teacher's body. The cat head-butted its owner. Its purr was getting louder and louder.

It seemed like an age before Ms Martinet's head slowly lifted. Her hands clutched the furry body, then began to stroke it. She blinked slowly. When she opened her eyes again, they were focused.

'...That's Noodles... She was lost. Is she alright?'

'Hello Miss. So that's why you were talking to Badpenny about noodles. I think she's OK, though she's had a bit of a scare,' Milly said.

'She's injured! Look – she's bleeding. I need to tend to her immediately. If I find out that it was Badpenny who hurt her...' Ms Martinet's fingers curled into claws. 'I assume you can find your own way out?'

Clutching Noodles to her heart and staggering slightly, Ms Martinet hurried away. Herman Blight scurried after her. 'I know the quickest way out, Ms Martinet,' he called. When he reached her, he tried to put a supportive arm around her shoulders. She batted him away like an annoying fly.

'Well done, Mills. No one else would have thought of a Cat Cure. Do you think it's permanent?' Charlie said.

Milly smiled at the nickname. She liked it. 'Don't know. Let's hope so. Badpenny was right – Ms Martinet was beyond *human* help! If anything could reach her, it was going to be a cat. Now we just need to make sure the headphones are safe and then...' She stopped and slapped a hand to her forehead.

'We're idiots! We've left the headphones with Badpenny. We've got to get them before she can move!'

Edgar Borgia's pale face went paler. He looked at his watch. 'Do you know, I'd forgotten that I had a meeting with Miss Vipond tonight. I'd better be off!'

With more of a grimace than a smile, he scuttled away.

'Great. Thanks, Sir. You leave us to face the mad evil genius by ourselves!' Charlie muttered.

'Never trust a man who teaches lying. The hour's just about up. Come on, Charlie.'

-oOo-

With Wolfie lighting the way and Gruffles bounding around him, Milly and Charlie ran back to where they'd left Badpenny. Her prison had dissolved. She was gone, leaving the enamelled handcuffs lying open on the ground. And she'd taken the headphones with her.

'Too late!' Charlie groaned. '*How* did she get out of those handcuffs?'

'Do you remember Agatha saying that she was related to lots of escapologists? I bet Badpenny is her aunt or her third cousin or something.' Milly said, angrily. 'Loads of criminal families are related to each other! I should have thought of that!'

'Where would she go? How did we miss her?' Charlie asked.

'I expect she just took another way out. She said there are doors everywhere! She'll go straight after Ms Martinet. Badpenny hates her even more than Miss Vipond hates Cubs and Brownies. She's obsessed with proving she's better than her – it's all she cares about. This time, she'll get her. And then she'll come after us. She won't want us raising the alarm. Come on!' Milly took to her heels, with Charlie following close behind her.

It seemed to take a long time to retrace their footsteps. Too long. They pelted through countless tunnels. One of them split into two, with the branches heading in opposite directions. 'I didn't notice this when we were coming down here. Did you?" Charlie asked.

Milly shook her head. 'No. Maybe we passed it after Badpenny captured us. We were too busy listening to her and wondering what was happening to worry about where we were going. Or maybe we're just lost.'

'Any idea which way we're supposed to go?' asked Charlie.

'Nope. And there's no time to worry about it. Badpenny reckons there's doors everywhere. Let's hope she was right!' Without further hesitation, she ran down the right-hand fork of the tunnel. Charlie, Wolfie and Gruffles followed.

It didn't take long to come across a door. It hadn't been closed properly. The light generated by Wolfie showed that it was made from long, vertical boards. 'A bit like the back of a cupboard,' Charlie said, pushing it.

They passed through it and then through another, shallower space before emerging into a room they knew.

Ms Martinet's office. The little group rushed to the door. Charlie tugged the handle but it wouldn't budge.

'Locked,' he groaned. 'Badpenny, I suppose, trying to make life difficult for us.'

'Maybe. Or it could have been Mrs Christie, on her nightly rounds. Who knows? We could get Wolfie to try to break the door down, I suppose, but the anti-theft devices on it are legendary. It could take him a while, and attract a lot of unwelcome attention.' Milly turned on the light and looked around for something – anything – that might help them.

It took no time at all to spot something on Ms Martinet's desk that she hadn't seen before. A slim, upright slab was protruding through a slit in the granite. Some kind of screen or monitor.

Charlie reached it first. The screen was blank but warm, as if it had just been switched off. 'It'll be protected, but there isn't a password in existence that my personal password tracker can't sniff out! I call it HOLMES. Like Sherlock.' He produced his mobile and a short connector, and linked them to the screen.

It only took a few seconds. Words and letters began flickering across the mobile's display, so fast that it was impossible to take them in. Suddenly they stopped at the word *MITTENS*. The upright screen flickered to life.

'*Mittens*? Why mittens?' Milly wondered.

Charlie shrugged and unplugged his mobile. 'Maybe she's got cold hands?'

The black and white image on the screen was of the front gates, looking outwards towards the Dependable world. The headlights of a car flashed by. Around the edge of the screen were other little images of other parts of the school – the Library, the Dining Room, the classrooms, the outbuildings, the woods and many others.

'I *knew* that tree was weird! There must be loads of cameras, all scattered around the school,' Milly said. 'I suppose Badpenny was using them to track down Ms Martinet. You need to find both of them, quickly.'

Charlie flicked expertly through the images, enlarging and then reducing each one in turn.

'This is state-of-the-art technology! Must've cost the school a fortune,' he said. And then: 'There! There's Ms Martinet. Out in the woods.'

-oOo-

Milly and Charlie watched as Griselda Martinet made her way through the trees, still cradling Noodles. It looked as if she'd shaken off Herman Blight. She headed for the furthest outbuilding and opened the door.

Another hidden camera took over. This one was located inside the building that Ms Martinet had just entered. She turned on the light and opened a dusty filing cabinet that looked like it had been dumped there a long time ago. She pulled out a metal box. There were indistinct symbols on the lid.

Charlie squinted at the monitor. 'What's that? Can't quite make it out...'

Milly peered too. 'I think it's – yes – a cross – probably red. Medicine! And the other symbol – I think it's meant to be a cat, with a floppy paw. Aha, feline first aid,' Milly said, with a quick smile.

After tending to Noodles' injury, the Head Teacher replaced the box and from another drawer, removed a folded blanket. She put it on the floor, plumped it up and nestled the cat into it. Then she turned off the light and left the outbuilding, leaving the door ajar. Yet another camera tracked her through the trees.

Suddenly she stopped and began peering all around her. 'She must've heard something,' Milly muttered.

They saw a thin white hand appear out of the gloom behind the teacher.

'Look out!' Charlie yelled, uselessly.

The hand grabbed Ms Martinet's shoulder and she sprang backwards. The wide white forehead and dark curls of Edgar Borgia appeared out of the darkness. Ms Martinet made a lunge for his throat and then seemed to stop herself. She planted her hands on her hips. Her mouth was moving forcefully. 'She's having a go at him,' Milly said, smiling.

Borgia cringed and tried to turn away, but Ms Martinet grabbed him by the arm. She began to haul him through the trees.

'Charlie, look!' Milly was pointing at one of the small pictures around the edge of the screen. Quickly, Charlie enlarged it. It showed another part of the woods – it was impossible to pinpoint exactly where. Pecunia Badpenny was creeping between the trees, peering in every direction.

Badpenny came to halt. She rubbed her gloved hands together and tiptoed away to the right of the screen. 'Hellfire, I think she's found her!' Charlie groaned.

Milly was already running back through the kitten cupboard. 'Come on, we've got to find another way out of here.'

-oOo-

In the maze of tunnels, Milly, Charlie, Wolfie and Gruffles came to a halt at a gaping door that they hadn't noticed before. *No wonder we didn't see it – stuck in that dark corner. And it's half the size of the other doors,* Milly thought.

Looking closely, they could make out some faded graffiti above the door, written in elaborate script: '*B de B's personal emergency egress. Lesser Brothers are forbidden from using this door, on pain of death.*' Next to the warning was a neat drawing of someone in knee breeches dangling from a scaffold, with his tongue hanging out.

'Charming! What's an egress? A female eagle?' Charlie asked. 'Do you think Sir Bryon had a secret pet, like me?'

Milly groaned. 'Do you know, I sometimes think that Gruffles' idiocy must be catching? I hate to disappoint you, but it's just an old-fashioned word for an exit. Come on!'

CHAPTER TWENTY-EIGHT

They found themselves in another, very different room. It was a little wider than most of the other rooms, and long ago it had been luxuriously furnished. But the fabric on the chaise longue that was pushed against the wall had faded to a colour so nondescript that Milly couldn't put a name to it. The candle sconces above it managed only the faintest glint of their original glowing gold.

Charlie blew the cobwebs off a tarnished mirror, all carved leaves and grimy cherubs. He huffed onto the glass and pulled the sleeve of his burglar's top over his hand, then used it to wipe away the mildew covering the mirror's surface. When he'd cleared a space, he peered at himself. 'The last person to look in this mirror was probably Sir Bryon de Bohun. Quite creepy, when you think about it,' he said, quietly.

Milly was blowing cobwebs from an ancient champagne bottle. It had been lying on the floor, next to a broken wineglass. 'I wonder if this is the bottle that killed him?'

She turned it over in her hands. 'Look there's still some champagne in it. Although it's changed into a sort of gunge, over the years. And there's some dusty fingerprints on it. Maybe they're his butler's.' She put the bottle down almost reverently and continued inspecting the room.

The only other item of interest was a wooden case, now open to reveal a pristine red velvet interior. Although it was empty, the fabric still bore the impression of a long-barrelled pistol and half a dozen little round indentations, where the bullets had nestled.

There was another door at the far end of the room, smaller than average. It had been left open. Through it Milly and Charlie could see the silhouettes of dozens of trees.

'So that's how Badpenny got out so fast. She must have gone into Ms Martinet's office to check the cameras and come back this way. It's a lot faster than running all through the school. Safer too. And – some more bad news – it looks like Badpenny's pinched his gun!' Milly said, leading the way through the door and out into the woods.

They ran on.

A couple of minutes later, Milly, Charlie, Gruffles and Wolfie came to a halt. They were in the densest, darkest part of the wood. Somewhere not far away they'd heard a sound, as if something quite big had hit the ground. Wolfie's ear probes were upright and quivering. His body swung in the direction of the noise. Milly patted his chilly rump: 'Off you go!'

Wolfie streaked towards the noise, eyes blazing. The others dashed after him.

It was impossible to keep pace with him. There were trees to dodge, darkness to hamper them, tree roots and clusters of plants to trip them up. Ahead of them, out of sight, Milly and Charlie heard a squeal as Wolfie ambushed his prey. A second or two later, they caught up. Wolfie was hovering over a prone figure.

'Milly Dillane and Charlie Partridge, what in Hades do you think you're doing, setting that creature on me?' Miss Vipond spluttered. 'You'd better have a good explanation or you'll be off to the nearest Accident and Emergency Department. I was waiting for a – friend – when I tripped over these worthless roots.' She glared at the roots as if they'd done it on purpose.

She stood up and dusted down her dress. Her severe bun was disintegrating, and wisps of hair were straggling over her face. 'The next thing I know, this space-age Rottweiler appears out of nowhere and starts menacing me! Are you trying to use shock tactics to prove you're not completely useless?'

Milly managed to bite back an apology. 'It's not you we're trying to menace, Miss. It's Badpenny. She's plotting to destroy the school and wipe Ms Martinet's brain. We need to stop her before she finds Ms Martinet. She's out here, somewhere, looking after a cat... burglar.'

'A cat burglar? In Blaggard's woods? You're either a dribbling fool or you're hallucinating. As for you, Charlie Partridge, I should've expected some form of idiocy from you. Mrs Christie was telling me you've started eating dog food! I'm taking you both back to your rooms. You can explain yourselves to Ms Martinet in the morning. Now, let me pick up my marking...'

As Miss Vipond bent down, Wolfie launched himself at her, knocking her flat again. Charlie opened his mouth to protest, but Wolfie had already whizzed past the furious teacher and was dodging through the trees with the ease of a dragonfly on a reed-choked lake.

Milly, Charlie and Gruffles followed as best they could.

CHAPTER TWENTY-NINE

Milly came to a stop behind a tree and craned around it, trying to control her breathing. Charlie and Gruffles were some distance away, lost in the woods. Judging from the noises coming from them, they'd just collided and were untangling themselves. She had no idea where Wolfie was.

Pecunia Badpenny was cramming the Hay-Zee headphones over Edgar Borgia's head.

'Mercy, Ms Badpenny! I have an aged grandmother and eleven orphans to support,' Borgia quavered. 'Granny's on her last legs. And several of the orphans are feeling peaky, too!'

'Spare me your pathetic Fabrications, you witless worm. I'm doing the world a favour, brainwashing you,' Badpenny spat at him. She flicked on the headphones. Immediately Borgia crumpled to the ground in a senseless heap.

'Faugh! A deeply inferior brain. I've calculated that even your average Dependable should take several seconds to brainwash.'

She beckoned Ms Martinet with the pistol. 'Come here, Griselda. I hope you're thinking about something pleasant, because it's the last thought you'll have. I've given up on the idea of enslaving you. I just want you dead.'

Darting looks of sheer hatred in Badpenny's direction, the Head Teacher had no choice but to comply.

'That's it... nice and slowly. Now pick up those headphones and turn off the volume dial. I want the pleasure of switching it on, myself. Now put them on. You may wish to close your eyes. No? You've got courage, I'll say that for you. Goodbye, Griselda,' Badpenny crooned.

Badpenny's gloved hand touched the volume button. Milly took a deep breath and launched herself forwards.

And then a cold, heavy object flew past her and cannoned into Badpenny. As the villain flew backwards she stared into Wolfie's yellow eyes and heard his 'Perp!' of joy. The sound changed to one of dismay as Wolfie thwacked into a tree. He tumbled to the ground, the light in his eyes flickering from yellow to green. Then it went out.

Griselda Martinet swayed, then crumpled onto the grass. Milly reached her. Badpenny, too, crashed into a tree. For a second she sat on the ground, dazed. Then she scrambled forward, stretching for the gun. Her gloved fingers clawed it at for a second, then grabbed it. She pointed it at Griselda Martinet. Milly stepped in front of the teacher, shielding her.

Badpenny shook her head and sighed. 'You again! Move aside, Milly Dillane. Just walk back into the school and get on with your life. I'll even let you and your lanky sidekick leave Blaggard's when I take over as Head, instead of destroying you. Go now.'

As she spoke, Badpenny cocked the pistol.

Milly looked at it, straining her ears to locate her friends. There was no sign of Wolfie, but Charlie was crashing around and calling to her, some distance away. Too far away to help. *I should've begged Agatha Quint for those escapology tips. Too late now,* Milly thought.

'You're wondering if the gun works?' Badpenny asked. 'Let's find out shall we?'

Milly looked compellingly into Badpenny's eyes, willing her not to glance towards Wolfie. His tails were starting to lift and the glow in his eyes had returned, although he was still sprawled at a wonky angle.

'Last chance, Milly Dillane. Move away now or take the consequences.'

Milly shook her head. 'I'll take the consequences. Everyone will tell you – Betrayal's one of my worst subjects.'

Badpenny tutted. 'You wretched Dependable! I was Fabricating, anyway. Just to see what you'd do. Of course I'm going to shoot you. I'm looking forward to it. I only wish someone was around to record it so I could put it on Crimbook.'

She pulled the trigger.

Just as a flash of fire was erupting from the end of the pistol, a ball of blinding energy hurled itself over Badpenny, the gun and the bullet. All three froze, the bullet floating as if it was suspended from an invisible thread. The fire streaking from the barrel of the pistol was frozen too and it hung in the air like sleeping lightning.

Milly's legs gave way but before she could fall Wolfie was there, propping her up. Milly gave him a fierce hug. 'Thank you. You may not wear tights and a cape, but you're still a super-hero!' Wolfie looped a wobbly loop before soaring into the cone of light and gulping down the bullet with a satisfied *perp*.

Charlie caught up and rushed to Ms Martinet. Jane Vipond, arriving late on the scene, spotted Edgar Borgia on the ground and dropped to her knees beside him with a little moan.

Milly pulled out her mobile, took some photos of the helpless Badpenny and gave her a wide smile.

'I know you can hear me. You call yourself a criminal mastermind, but from where I'm standing you look more like something that a cat's finished playing with. You like publicity, don't you? You should be pleased, then, because we're gonna make you really famous. Not infamous, but famous as in "Hey, it's that stupid woman who thought she was a super crim, but got beaten by a couple of kids".'

Badpenny's eyes gleamed with fury. 'You were talking about Crimbook just now. Give these photos a few minutes on there and they'll go viral,' Milly continued. 'I'm sending them now.' She pressed the SEND button on her mobile. 'Pretty soon, you won't be Badpenny any more, you'll be Sadpenny.'

Charlie grinned at his friend. 'Remember when we were talking about stealing someone's reputation? That's exactly what we've done!'

Milly smiled at him, then turned and led the way back to the main building. Jane Vipond was enthusiastically

160

slapping Borgia's face, to revive him. He groaned and opened his eyes. She pulled him to his feet and helped him away. Ms Martinet snatched the headphones from her head and started to stumble after Miss Vipond, with Charlie supporting her. Gruffles and Wolfie chased each other through the trees, without a care in the world.

From her glowing prison, Badpenny's eyes followed the little group, promising mayhem and murder.

CHAPTER THIRTY

At breakfast the next morning Ms Martinet caused astonished murmurs by coming *in person* to the Dining Room and asking Milly and Charlie to accompany her to her office. They were happy to go because they had lots of questions for her, but their fellow Year Sevens expected the worst. Agatha Quint gave them a twisted smile, as if she didn't know whether to gloat or sympathise. William Proctor dropped his Encyclopaedia of Crime (A – AAM) into his porridge and looked genuinely regretful at the prospect of the pair's expulsion from Blaggard's.

On another table, Jet Mannington had been talking earnestly to a bored looking Sixth Form girl. As the little group passed him he looked up. 'Good luck in the Chamber of Horrors. You'll need it!' he called, with a glance at his companion.

Milly flashed him a sarcastic grin. 'Cheers, Jet. We'll keep our eyes open for buckets of ice-cold water.' Jet's smirk dissolved. The Sixth Former lifted a hand to her face to hide her smile. Ms Martinet beamed her approval.

As Milly and Charlie tried to settle in Ms Martinet's knobbly chairs, the Head Teacher cleared her throat. 'First, I must thank you for ruining Badpenny's plan. My recollection of last night is hazy, but I know that it's not only me that you've saved. Just imagine what she'd do with an army of mindless slaves. The whole country would be under her thumb! You've certainly proved that you have courage and determination.'

She looked at Charlie. 'Mr Partridge, I've no doubt that Miss Dillane has informed you of my concerns about her suitability for Blaggard's. You're included in those doubts.'

Charlie grimaced and nodded.

'While I've yet to see proof that your criminal motivation has improved, you've got the better of Badpenny,' Ms Martinet continued. 'That's enough to guarantee your places at Blaggard's, while we try to make you into criminals. Look on it as a stay of execution, if you like.'

'Thank you, Miss!' Charlie grinned. 'How's Mr Borgia?'

'He was lucky. At the very moment Badpenny flicked the switch on the headphones, he fainted. That saved him. He has regained his mind, such as it is, except the memory of last night. It's better that he doesn't remember that. I don't want anyone to know how close Badpenny came to beating me, and Mr Borgia isn't known for his discretion.'

'What about Miss Vipond? Will she keep things secret?' Milly asked.

'She will. I've had to bribe her by making her Head of Defiance and Discourtesy. As she's our only teacher of those subjects, it's not a huge sacrifice.' Just for a second, the Head Teacher looked a little regretful.

'You may not be surprised to learn that I am seeking a new teacher of Advanced Hacking,' she continued. 'Mrs Prye confessed that she was in Badpenny's pay – she supplied her with all sorts of information about what was going on here, and ran errands for her. I've sacked her and ensured that she'll find it *ab-so-lutely* impossible to get another criminal job. She'll have to go straight!'

'Ouch! Actually, we know someone who might be interested in her job,' Milly said. 'What's happened to Badpenny?'

'I hired some henchmen via the Pros and Cons website.' Ms Martinet looked gleeful. 'If I'd been feeling less unwell, I'd have sorted her out myself, but never mind. Dreams seldom come true. Anyway, their service was excellent. The henchmen arrived almost immediately, and were waiting when Badpenny's prison dissolved... It's a shame that her Wolf has disappeared, by the way. What an asset he would be! He'd quell a food fight in microseconds! And think of the punishments he could inflict! I don't suppose you have any idea where he is?' She darted a look of challenge at Milly and Charlie.

Milly had anticipated the question. She opened her eyes wide and shook her head. 'No, we haven't seen him since last night.' *It's almost true. He's been in invisibility mode since then, so we haven't actually seen him, even though he spent the night in Charlie's room, playing tricks on Gruffles.*

'Hmmm,' Ms Martinet looked less than convinced. 'Anyway, the stooges bundled Badpenny into the back of a lorry, took her to a leaky container ship and locked her in the hold. The crew are under orders to drop her off in China, eventually. It may take a quite few months. She gets horribly seasick, you know. She always has.' Ms Martinet heaved a deep, satisfied sigh. 'I've informed the Chinese government that she's been poaching their pandas. They're *very* keen to get their hands on her. The crew were a dodgy bunch too, so they may just decide to drop her into the ocean. One way or another, she's toast!'

So much for Ms Martinet not being malicious. 'I suppose she deserves it. Was Noodles alright after her adventure?' Milly wanted to know next.

'Yes, thank you. I should explain, in the strictest confidence, that Noodles is the great-great-great-great-granddaughter of the cat that brought me up when my mother abandoned me as a baby. I think you may have spotted her photo in my secret cupboard? I'd have died if it hadn't been for Mittens.'

At the mention of the cat's name, Milly and Charlie exchanged a glance. 'So that's how you picked the password for your desk monitor!' Charlie said.

'Rest assured, I'll be changing it as soon as you leave!' Ms Martinet looked annoyed. 'Anyway, I see it as my criminal duty to thank Mittens by looking after her descendants. Incidentally, Badpenny was wrong – I knew there was a secret door behind my little shrine. Sometimes I let my feline charges go for a wander there. What I didn't know was the extent of the tunnels. Or that Badpenny was using them. The cheek of that woman is endless! At least it was.' She looked at her watch. 'She's gone now. Or will be, soon enough.' She gave a little cough. 'Perhaps we should discuss your reward for keeping my love of cats to yourselves?'

'Nothing, Miss. We won't tell,' Milly said, after a quick glance at Charlie.

'Nothing? How unBlaggardian! Mr Partridge, I'm aware that your dog is an illegal resident here. Perhaps I can thank you by offering him a permanent home at Blaggard's? It'll be strictly between us. Having a phantom hound gives us a certain distinction. Crumley's has nothing like it! In fact, I'm considering including it in the school prospectus. Although it's a pity that he's a Poodle – something massive and drooling would be a lot better.'

'He's not a Poodle, Miss. He's a Spangle. But that would be brilliant, thank you,' grinned Charlie.

Ms Martinet looked blank. 'I have *ab-so-lutely* no idea what you're talking about.' She stood up. 'It's time for Assembly. Any more questions?'

Milly had one more. 'What happened to the headphones? Are they safe? I'd hate to think what would happen if someone found them lying around. Although there are certain people around here I'd like to use them on. Just for a second.'

'I had the same thought. Don't worry – they're safe. Somewhere I can easily put my hand on them if anyone annoys me too much.'

Turning to close the door on the way out of Ms Martinet's office, Milly had a final glimpse of the terrifying Head. She'd sat down again, pulled open a drawer in her desk and extracted a fuzzy tortoiseshell kitten. After settling it on her shoulder, she was tickling it under the chin and talking nonsense to it.

You won't scare anyone if you're mooning over a fluffy kitten, thought Milly, remembering the words from the school prospectus that she'd read aloud to Charlie on their first day at Blaggard's.

CHAPTER THIRTY-ONE

There was time for a quick chat as Milly and Charlie walked to the Assembly Hall. 'How are you feeling, Mills? About the "stay of execution"? Are you glad?'

Milly cocked her head and thought about it. '...Yes. YES! You know what? It's been fun. Some of it. Most of it. I bet no other school gives you the chance to chase super-villains through hidden tunnels and befriend robot dogs! Not even Crumley's!'

And definitely not those boring Dependable schools, she thought. *I think it's going to be OK here. I think I can be myself. All I need to do is persuade Ms Martinet that I'm getting more villainous. Which I won't be. Still, I like a challenge.*

'Me, too,' Charlie replied. 'And I get to keep Gruffles with me! All this adventuring's helped with my decision-making, too.' After a moment he added, 'At least, I think it has... *Why* are you laughing?'

When Milly had regained her composure, he said, 'Just wait till I see Miss Vipond. I'm going to be so rude to her!

I'll use the Burglar's Underpants insult – I know that one works!'

Milly punched his arm and the pair merged with the other Blaggardians who were filing into the hall. Ms Martinet appeared on stage. She raised one hand. All talk stopped.

'Good morning, tyrants of tomorrow. I have some serious news for you. Overnight, a plot to destroy the school has been thwarted. You'll be shocked to learn that the plotter was Pecunia Badpenny, and even more so when I reveal that she was outwitted by two of our own students, and Year Sevens at that... Blaggard's owes its continued existence to Milly Dillane and Charlie Partridge.'

Ms Martinet led a round of applause. From every corner of the Assembly Hall, eyes were swivelling to stare at the unexpected heroes. Charlie shuffled his long limbs and smiled at those nearest to him. Milly lifted her head and stared right back.

'Yes, thank you, Miss Dillane and Mr Partridge. Obviously, Badpenny is unsuitable to lead the new school House. I'm tempted to say "I told you so", but that would be beneath me.' She paused for a moment. 'Actually, forget that. I told you so!

'Back to naming the new school house – the honour now shifts to the second most popular choice. As I am sure you will remember, that was Martinet.' She smiled at William Proctor. He blushed.

'So, it's up to me to appoint the new House Captain. I've decided, after much thought, to appoint one of the school's most dedicated wrongdoers – Jet Mannington.' There was a brief smatter of applause. Jet struggled to look cool. The squirm of his lips, as he tried to subdue his grin, reminded Milly of two worms that had been tied together at both ends.

'However, as Mr Mannington is known for his over-enthusiasm, especially when it comes to trying to impress girls and pushing younger students around, I've also decided to appoint a Vice-Captain. Two, in fact, to ensure that Mr Mannington's new power doesn't go to his well-tended head. The Vice-Captains will be ... Milly Dillane and Charlie Partridge.' Glancing at the pair, Ms Martinet raised her eyebrows in challenge.

Milly looked at Charlie. His face was rigid with surprise, making him look like the taxidermed Sir Bryon. 'Well, we'll get loads of chances to annoy Jet. Might as well start now!' Milly said to him, in an undertone.

She turned to Jet with a wide smile. 'It'll be lovely, working so closely together. In no time at all, we'll be *best friends*,' she cooed. Jet looked as if he'd rather sew his own eyelids shut.

Ms Martinet was getting ready to leap down from the stage. 'That's all for now. I'll leave you to congratulate the new House Captain and his deputies, and to prepare for tomorrow's Lightfinger Trophy presentations. Any questions?'

Charlie grabbed Milly's arm. 'We've forgotten the trophy. We've saved the school but doomed ourselves. We'll be expelled tomorrow after all, and thrown to the Crumley's wolves. Unless we can present Badpenny's ruined reputation on a golden plate or something?'

'Relax, Charlie.' Milly's eyes were shining. 'It's all under control.'

CHAPTER THIRTY-TWO

I t was Grand Submission Day for the Lightfinger Trophy and Blaggard's was buzzing.

Miss Vipond had swapped her grey dress for one splattered with giant orange and purple flowers, with vines coiling around them like hungry snakes. Agatha Quint became so excited that she mislaid her handcuffs and, according to William Proctor, Griselda Martinet was heard humming a popular love song on the way to Assembly.

The presentation of entries was due to start at midday. Blaggardians re-formed into their groups and set about ensuring that their entry looked fabulous. All around the school students were huddling, brandishing dusters and cans of polish. Nick Lightfinger was everywhere – fussing over the windows in the Assembly Hall, sticking his blunt nose into the groups of busy students and even poking around the Twisted Gates.

The only Blaggardians who seemed to be immune from the frenzy of preparation were Milly and Charlie. As lessons were suspended, they spent the morning in the Library, updating their Crimbook accounts and playing video games. Charlie had a new game – *Tea With the Vicar* – and it was all the rage at Blaggard's. Participants had to bake virtual cakes, arrange flowers and twigs in assorted vases and help grannies across the road (ignoring the impulse to abandon them in the middle) before entertaining an elderly cleric with appropriate conversation. Blaggardians found it perplexing but hilarious and Charlie was enjoying trying to concoct the most disgusting cake imaginable, in an effort to make the virtual vicar lose his temper.

Miss Grimbly looked up from her work to see what they were up to. She rubbed at her false eyelashes. 'What's that flickering in the air above you?' she asked.

'What? Where?' Milly asked, peering around with a look of puzzled innocence.

The Librarian looked again. 'Oh. Nothing. I must have imagined it. I've probably picked up a slight concussion after my late-night Kung Fu knockout class.' She returned to the book that she was enthusiastically shrouding in plastic.

By 11.45, students were jostling to get into the Assembly Hall. As Charlie took up his place, nowhere near the stuffed Sir Bryon, he went over proceedings in his mind. *Everything's under control. Milly's at the back, keeping Wolfie quiet. I just go and join her when it's our turn. I'll let her do the talking.* He peered over the sea of heads, seeking reassurance from Milly. She met his eyes and gave him a cheerful smile.

As the Great Clock of Blaggard began to strike midday, the Hall's double doors were thrown open. A thin man prowled in. He wore inky dark glasses and his hair was slicked back against his skull. *His suit's so sharp you could slice cucumbers with it*, Charlie thought.

'Look, it's...' someone called out.

'Isn't that...?'

The man sauntered to the stage, where Nick Lightfinger and a flushed Ms Martinet waited to greet him. With these formalities out of the way, the man removed his sunglasses with his back to the crowd, then swivelled round. The crowd went wild.

'It's Gavin McGlintock! The Sneering Specialist,' a girl shouted, pretending to swoon.

Charlie's heart started hammering. Sweat prickled his palms and his back. He raised his eyes to the heavens and prayed that Milly's plan would work, and that he wouldn't be made to look like a total loser in front of his hero.

Ms Martinet stepped forward. 'Yes, it's a great honour to welcome Gavin McGlintock as our guest judge. No one knows more about valuing loot than him.'

Gavin McGlintock raised a hand. 'Hello, Blaggard's!' His voice was a low Scottish burr. 'I was delighted to be invited back to help. As Ms Martinet says, I'm the best in the business.'

McGlintock had been smiling his rare smile, but now his lips straightened. He paused for a second and then his expression became fierce. 'I'm just hoping – *really* hoping – that there'll be no reason for me to use my catchphrase –'

'*IT'S NOT WORTH THE WEAR ON YOUR CROWBAR!*' the crowd yelled.

The presentations began in a suitably fiendish manner.

Charlie watched open mouthed as Seth Daggersby, Captain of De Bohun House, clanked into the hall dressed in a suit of scarlet and black Samurai armour. With its iron scales and plates, and its domed helmet surmounted by long, golden horns, it reminded Charlie of a giant, malevolent beetle.

Surrounded by his proud team, Seth described their operation to steal the armour. 'It belonged to a mad millionaire who keeps it in a vault under a volcano. He'd agreed to lend it to the Museum of Creepy and Disgusting Stuff in London. We went to the museum disguised as Dependable school kids. Naomi here pretended to be dying from a snake bite, from the Creepy Creatures Enclosure.'

Naomi briefly reprised her performance.

'Then, while everyone was fussing over her, I grabbed it and dragged it over to a window.' Seth pointed to the final member of their group – a Year Ten called Tom. 'Tom was outside with a trampoline. He bounced up and grabbed it and ran off with it. It was a real team effort!'

There was a storm of applause. Seth's team lapped it up like one of Ms Martinet's kittens with a saucer of milk.

Object after fabulous object was exhibited to the judges. Magnificent jewellery, opulent paintings, an ancient sword, an Egyptian mummy and a jewelled orb were among the riches being presented, as the Blaggardians gasped and applauded. Nick Lightfinger could barely suppress his glee. He picked up the orb and caressed it greedily.

After each presentation the judges huddled together to agree a value. Then Lightfinger announced it and Edgar Borgia noted it down, with Miss Vipond peering crossly over his shoulder to make sure he wasn't tempted to Fabricate. The submissions were then placed on or, in the case of the larger ones, next to a purple-draped table by the stage.

At one stage, two of the big windows that extended from the floor up to the ceiling had to be opened, with the help of a handheld remote in Agatha Quint's hand.

No sooner had the windows slid apart than Jezebel Jackson roared into the Hall in a streamlined Buggatini, all crimson and chrome. It was one of the world's most valuable cars. She screeched to a halt mere inches from the audience. Many of the spectators shrieked and jumped back. Then the room went wild. Through the car's open window, Charlie saw Jezebel grinning wickedly.

After backing the Buggatini against one wall, Jezebel jumped out and joined the rest of her team. 'We stole it from a locked garage on a moat inside a high walled compound. It was being patrolled by about a hundred armed security guards – all ex-SAS,' she explained. 'There were masses of alarms to disable, too. Agatha got through everything – the guards, the locks *and* the alarms. It was touch and go, but we did it.' Agatha grinned and basked in the applause.

After a brief consultation, the Buggatini was announced to be worth fifteen million pounds. This was the most valuable object so far.

At last it was Jet's team's turn. Shady Mannington and William Proctor made their way to the front of the hall, lugging a wooden plinth between them. Then Jet strutted in. He was carrying a fat book on a golden cushion. Charlie saw the subtle sheen of pearls embedded in the book's binding. The crowd went silent.

'Ms Martinet, Nick, Gavin, I present to you – the only existing copy of Sir Thomas Blaggard's book – *From Pongy Peasante to Stinking Rich Rascal – My Rise to ye Toppe of ye Criminal Underworlde*,' Jet read the title carefully, before lowering the cushion onto the plinth.

'It was nearly impossible to steal,' he continued, with a smirk. 'We had to pinch an armoured car before we could even try it. Then, after we'd used the car to knock down the doors to the vault, I had to jump over about a million lethal lasers, designed to cut burglars in half, and do a quick cartwheel round a camera that took photos of the vault every second, while disguised as a nun. The others helped too. A bit,' he waved a vague hand at William Proctor and Shady.

Charlie saw doubt on the faces of William Proctor and Shady Mannington. *I reckon at least half of that's pure Fabrication. They'd contradict him, if they dared.*

Ms Martinet's mouth formed an 'O'. She couldn't resist jumping down to stroke the book. 'Mr Mannington, I'm overwhelmed. How can we possibly place a value on this?' she faltered. After another lingering look, she went into a huddle with Lightfinger and Gavin McGlintock.

Charlie held his breath as the judges argued over the book's value. He became aware that absolute silence had fallen over the Hall. Every ear seemed to be tuned into the judges' whispered conversation. Eventually Ms Martinet nodded and stepped back.

Lightfinger came to the front of the stage to announce:

'The value of Sir Thomas Blaggard's autobiography is ... *eighteen million pounds!*'

The audience went bananas. Jet, Shady and William Proctor glowed. Charlie gulped and wished he was a million miles away. Or trussed up and thrown down a mineshaft. Or anywhere at all, except standing in the Hall at Blaggard's, waiting to be humiliated in front of the Sneering Specialist and several hundred merciless tyrants-in-training.

Finally, the applause died down.

'We've reached our final submission,' Nick Lightfinger said, flatly. 'Don't get your hopes up – despite their recent astounding luck in outdoing Badpenny, I've seen no sign of potential in either of them in *my* subject. It's Milly Dillane and Charlie Partridge.'

CHAPTER THIRTY-THREE

From their separate vantage points, Milly and Charlie moved forward. They met near the middle of the Hall.

'Ready?' Milly said quietly.

'I suppose so. As ready as I'll ever be.'

When they reached Lightfinger, he gave them a tiny, contemptuous smile. 'Well? Where is it? Surely you managed to feloniously acquire *something?*'

'Yes, Sir. Do you want to see it?' Milly asked.

'Let me think.' Lightfinger made a show of scratching his head, as if he was pondering a difficult question. 'YES! I'd really like to see it NOW, if that's OK with you?'

'You heard him, Wolfie, he wants to see you.'

The Wolf appeared. Just like that. One moment he wasn't there. The next he was, floating so close to Lightfinger that he stirred his mousy hair. The light in the Wolf's eyes pulsed blackly. Its whole body glowed. It shot shards of white energy through the open windows. Gasps and little screams rang out.

Milly gazed around the room at the awestruck faces.

Jet's not the only one who can Fabricate at short notice. No one's gonna contradict us. Badpenny will never confess that her own bodyguard turned against her to go and play with a smelly dog, even if she does survive Ms Martinet's plan. She'd be even more of a laughing stock than she already is. And Ms Martinet was so woozy, she won't remember what happened.

'You've all seen the Wolf before,' Milly said. 'We stole him from Badpenny. It was nearly impossible. She fought tooth and nail to keep him. She nearly shot us at least ten times. And she set a band of stooges onto us – '

'– Stooges. Dozens of them. They were massive. Some of them were drooling. They had axes.' Charlie corroborated, before adding, as an afterthought: 'And leopards on chains.'

'Thanks, Charlie.' Milly put a hand on her friend's shoulder. 'The Wolf's got powers you couldn't imagine. We've only seen a fraction of what he can do, and that's pretty terrifying! And he's unique – the only Wolf in the whole world. So what's he worth, Sir?'

When Wolfie had materialised, the Thievery teacher had cowered in a quivering beige heap. Now he seemed to pull himself together. 'Cheating!' he barked, stepping forward. 'That's cheating! No animals, it said in the rules. I'm expelling you! You're expelled.'

Ms Martinet had been watching from the stage. 'Mr Lightfinger! You're forgetting yourself. There's only one person who can expel Blaggardians, and it isn't you. It's debatable whether the Wolf is an animal at all, and I'm intrigued to see what it's worth. Come here and discuss it.'

Gavin McGlintock was busy assessing Wolfie. 'You'd be mad to disqualify this, Nick. Every tyrant in the world would pay any amount for it. You could name your own price,' he said, reaching a hand towards Wolfie to stroke him. Wolfie's eyes flashed red. The Sneering Specialist snatched back his hand. 'Definitely worth a load of wear on a shedload of crowbars!' His voice was full of awe.

Nick Lightfinger ignored Gavin McGlintock. For a second, he stared towards the open windows. Then he returned to glaring at Ms Martinet. 'You can't overrule me. I'm in charge of this competition. I thought of it!'

The Head Teacher's brows were drawn together like the hands of a clock at ten to two. 'Do you want to continue to work at Blaggard's, Mr Lightfinger? If so, I suggest you do as I say. Now.'

Lightfinger's face screwed into a puffy-cheeked ball. His fists curled.

'It's *my* competition. And my trophy,' he stormed. 'I'm not doing this any more.' He started to stomp away, the trophy dangling from one of his hands.

Milly turned to Charlie. 'That's weird. The iceberg has melted – just like that. He's up to something.'

Every eye followed the enraged teacher as he began barging his way through the crowd, shoving aside those who weren't quick enough to jump out of his way.

Then there was a flicker of movement in the very corner of Milly's field of vision. She jerked her head round to follow it. Two figures in scarecrow masks and camouflage jumpsuits were urgently stuffing the competition entries into large hessian sacks.

One of them dropped a tiara on the floor. As the figure bent to retrieve it, Milly caught a glimpse of a black and red uniform beneath the jumpsuit. *I know that uniform – they're from Crumley's!*

'Look!' Milly yelled, pointing. 'Thieves! Crumleians!'

She broke into a run. As she dashed towards the table, several things happened, almost simultaneously.

The Crumleian robbers swept as much of the portable swag as they could into their sacks. In their rush they knocked some of the treasures onto the floor. There wasn't time to retrieve them and they raced away. But they didn't dash towards the doors, as Milly expected. Instead, they headed for the Buggatini, which was still parked on the other side of the hall.

Nearly every Blaggardian – teacher and student – rushed towards them, bellowing their indignation.

'Get them!' someone yelled.

A voice Milly recognised – William Proctor's, she thought – called out: 'They're stealing our stolen goods! Stop them... Be on the look out for weapons, though!' That made people slow down a little.

Nick Lightfinger had been storming towards the doors, but suddenly he changed direction. He hurtled towards the Buggatini. He got there before the Crumleians and wrenched open the driver's door, dropping the Lightfinger Trophy as he did so. He jumped in and twisted the keys in the ignition. The car roared into ferocious life. Dozens of Blaggardians leapt out of its path.

The car skidded away, but it only went a dozen metres or so before Lightfinger braked sharply. 'Get in. NOW!' he yelled at the Crumleians, through the open driver's window.

The robbers pulled open the rear doors, threw in the bags of loot and scrambled in.

'Lightfinger's in league with the Crumleians!' someone yelled. 'He must have let them in through the Twisted Gates!' There were howls of outrage.

Meanwhile, Wolfie's attention had been distracted by a simpering photograph of a young Pecunia Badpenny. It was among a number of others on display under a yellowing placard that read *Annual Winners of the Blaggardian Most Likely To Stab You in the Back Competition*. Wolfie had knocked the photo onto the floor and was slowly incinerating it with a thin beam of light.

The noise and rush of movement seemed to bring Wolfie back to his senses. He spun round, assessed the situation for a millisecond and then hurtled forwards. He came to a halt just in front of the car.

With his passengers and the loot safely in the back of the Buggatini, Lightfinger once again stamped down on the accelerator.

Wolfie was already weaving one of his light prisons, but he was *just* a second too slow. The Buggatini smashed into him, sending him careering across the room, metal components spinning off him. He crashed into the stage and tumbled into a lifeless heap.

And then, instead of driving the car through the open windows towards freedom, Nick Lightfinger did something silly. He got out of the car and ran round in front of it. There, gleaming on the floor, was the jewelled orb that he'd clutched so greedily earlier on.

'Stupid man!' Milly muttered to herself, rushing to intercept him.

It was then that Agatha Quint, who was standing close by, blundered into Milly. 'Oh! Sorry!' she said, as Milly sprawled across the floor. Before she went down, Milly caught – or thought she'd caught – a little smile on Agatha's face.

Charlie was closer to the car. He slid across the polished wood floor, snatched up the orb and curled his long body around it. Lightfinger swore. He threw Charlie a murderous look and then dashed back to the car, where his Crumlcian accomplices were screaming at him to *HURRY UP!*

As Charlie was scrambling to his feet, holding the orb, Lightfinger was having a little trouble getting the car into gear. He crunched the gearbox horribly, making several people wince.

'Charlie, do something!' Milly yelled, as she got to her feet. She saw Agatha Quint merging back into the crowd. *Did she trip me on purpose? I'm gonna make sure that I find out,* Milly thought, fleetingly.

Charlie looked across at her and then down at the orb he was holding. He bounced it in his hand once, to assess its weight, before sending it spinning through the air. As it flew, the amethysts and rubies embedded in it reflected the sunshine, and red and purple glints danced around the Assembly Hall like reflections from a glitter ball. The orb sailed through the car's open window and caught the teacher on the side of his head, knocking him out.

Lightfinger's foot must have slipped off the accelerator as he lost consciousness, because the Buggatini came to a dramatic halt, against the wall. There was a tinkle of glass from a broken headlight, but, as far as Milly could see, it was otherwise unharmed.

The Crumleian robbers staggered out of the Buggatini. One of them pulled something from a pocket. It seemed to be a yellow tennis ball with a stalk like an apple. The robber whipped out a lighter and set fire to the stalk. Instantly, thick mustard-coloured smoke poured out of the ball, filling the room.

Leaving the loot in the back of the car and Nick Lightfinger to face the music, the Crumleians stumbled through the windows and out into the woods.

Inside the Hall there was a long moment of stunned silence, during which the sound of furious barks, and corresponding squeals of fear, told the Blaggardians that the ghost dog had found new victims.

Then the applause started. It came close the breaking the windows.

Charlie blushed. And then, instead of staring at the floor, as he'd have done only a week ago, he stood tall and beamed around the room. Milly felt a glow of pride in him.

Griselda Martinet had been issuing urgent instructions to the teaching staff. Milly made out the words 'clown' and 'at least ten years'. None too gently, the other teachers picked up the unconscious Lightfinger and dragged him away.

Ms Martinet scooped up the dented trophy, which was still lying on the floor where Lightfinger had dropped it. She carried it to Milly and Charlie.

'I'm not a great hugger. In fact, I haven't hugged a human

being for decades. But I *almost* feel like hugging you,' she said. 'You are deserving winners of the trophy, which will be changing its name immediately. Thank you.'

She gave the trophy to Milly and Charlie, one handle to each. When they held it high, the applause DID break the windows.

EPILOGUE

Every Saturday, the *Borage Bagpuize Gleaner* appeared in Blaggard's Library. It seldom had anything remarkable to report – ninety per cent of it was taken up with reports of Dependable jumble sales, stolen wheelbarrows and Ferrets in Need of a Good Home.

In the week after the Thievery competition fiasco, however, the paper contained an item of very interesting news.

STOLEN GOODS RETURNED TO RIGHTFUL OWNERS BY INVISIBLE HERO

Borage Bagpuize Police Station was inundated with phone calls last night from wealthy citizens. All reported being woken up by eerie lights and strange noises.

Upon investigation, they were amazed to find that their recently stolen possessions, many of great value, had been returned to their original resting places.

'The Moan'

'You could have knocked me down with a feather,' one resident, who prefers to remain anonymous, told our reporter. 'My beloved painting, Edwina Munch's 'The Moan' was back on the ballroom wall! What's the world coming to? It's enough to give you hope for the future!'

'Perps'

The mystery deepened when one citizen reported that, upon looking out of her bedroom window to investigate strange sounds that she described as 'perps,' she witnessed her stolen car, a valuable red Buggatini, floating down from the sky before being deposited back in its garage 'as if it was being controlled by an invisible driver. They've damaged the front headlight, but under the circumstances, I'm very grateful,' she said.

Reward!

The invisible benefactor, who has been nicknamed 'The See-Through Sentinel', is being hailed as a hero. The Gleaner is offering a substantial reward for information on the identity of this highly unusual crime fighter – a bus pass that will take you anywhere within a five mile radius FOR A WHOLE WEEK. How's that for generosity?

Milly snatched up the newspaper and took it to Charlie's room. She knocked urgently on his door.

'When you mended Wolfie, after his accident in the Hall, do you think you might have put some of his bits back in the wrong place?' she blurted out, as soon as Charlie's harassed face appeared round the door. 'He's doing some really weird stuff. He's taken all the loot back! Ms Martinet will be going bananas. The newspaper's saying that he's a hero. It's calling him "The See-Through Sentinel". He'll be saving Nick Lightfinger from his sentence as a clown on Children's Party Island next.'

'Oh great! Come in quickly. Shut the door behind you. Wolfie's completely out of control!'

Charlie jumped onto his bed. He teetered as he stretched upwards towards Wolfie, who'd attached himself to the ceiling. He gave the robot dog stern instructions.

'Wolfie, get him down. He's not used to being upside down. The blood will run to his head. He'll be sick, and I'm standing underneath him!'

Running around Wolfie and jumping over the light in the middle of the ceiling was Gruffles, alternately yapping excitedly and yelping in terror. 'Help me out, Mills,' begged Charlie.

'What do you expect me to do? If you can't reach him, I definitely can't! Why did you programme him to do that, anyway?' Milly managed to say, between gusts of laughter.

'Programme him to do this? You're kidding. He's doing it himself!'

At last Wolfie relented and gently wafted Gruffles back to the floor. Charlie collapsed onto his bed. Milly lay giggling on the floor, next to the panting Gruffles, who looked as if he'd never trust his legs again. Wolfie looped the loop, perping in excitement at the success of his prank.

'Do you think we'll ever have a normal day?' Charlie managed to ask, eventually.

'Not a hope,' said Milly Dillane with a wide smile.